Biff + wife

Alex

dog - Chester

Dr. Kneil

Interviewer ✓

Amelio - gang of x ✓

D'Angelo ✓
Crystal - gang of x
James - gang of x ✓
Brandon - gang of x ✓
Marie (Alex's #) ✓
Martha —
Triplets, Biff Jr, Doug, Jack

TERRELL NEWBY

GHOST OF PALMYRA HIGH

BASED ON ACTUAL PARANORMAL EVENTS

1619 Press
A Division of 1619 Consortium LLC
Nebraska

1619 Press August 2020

School Fiction/Horror

The Library of Congress has cataloged the 1619 Consortium edition as follows

Newby, Terrell, 1959---
Horror tales, America 1. Title.
(place the library of congress 2021946941
1619 Press ISBN: 978-1-66780-127-8
1619press.com

Printed in the United States of America

DEDICATION

Alex Ostiguin, a native son of the great cornhusker within the state of Nebraska, became a man at the age of 18 when he fathered his beautiful newborn daughter while still in high school. He went to Lincoln High School, taking his daughter to the school daycare while he attended classes, and worked late-night jobs to support his daughter before and after graduating.

Alex wrote his first horror essay in a composition class during the senior year. The first time he expressed his experiences working in a high school haunted by a ghost was at a writing class. Five years later, while working with his co-worker, the two shared ghost stories during a casual conversation. His co-worker Terrell Newby was researching ghost stories in Nebraska for a possible book when Alex shared his experience of working at a high school haunted by a ghost. After several lengthy conversations about his actual paranormal experiences at the high school, Newby asked Alex to provide context to the real experience. Thus, the story was fictionalized by his co-worker. Ninety per cent of his life experiences leading up to including the fictional accounts of his version were typed on his mobile phone, while the rest of the 10 per cent (the beginning accounts) were voiced on his phone and later translated.

Alex has always enjoyed horror and mystery books and films. He loves ice fishing in sub-zero weather in his ice tent. He and his brother have been known to fish for 24 hours straight, catching large catfish, bass, and a variety of Nebraska fish. During the cold winter months, they punch holes in icy lakes to catch fish.

PREFACE

Mystery books, mind-blowing thrillers, and stories with psychologically cathartic themes have fascinated me ever since I was young. When I decided to write this book, my inclination toward writing a thriller with hints of horror full of suspense and tragic events was understandable, as it came naturally to me.

After completing my first novel *Dragon Jester*, I began researching for my next book. It was while looking for actual paranormal ghost stories when ironically, I met a man named Alex who had lived through actual paranormal events. We connected, and I instantly began to work on *Ghost of Palmyra High*.

After six long months of researching and conversing with Alex, I was able to write most of the novel while at work during down periods or after work, often early mornings after midnight. Alex, the guy I asked to share his life experience leading to his hauntings while working as a janitor at the high school, shared his experiences one by one. The incidents he came across were discussed, recorded, and typed on most occasions. After months of editing and modifications, along with several other additions, I was eventually able to finish the story. Combining the actual experience and embellishing the story, giving it a fictional twist for the audience, gave me further courage to share this book with all the horror-lovers out there.

It goes without saying that my journey of writing *Ghost of Palmyra High* was not free of struggles or challenges. Regardless, I cherish every bit of it. That's because I believe that writing horror is a great vessel to be creative and entertaining. It is like riding a motorcycle; your mind is free to express and explore the unknown. This is my story, and I'm proudly sticking with it!

ABOUT THE AUTHOR

Terrell Newby was born in Chicago, Illinois. Growing up, he was greatly intrigued with the mysteries of *The Hardy Boys* book series, *Children of the Knight* by John Blackburn, *Dark Shadow* and " horror programs. Ever since, the author has been drawn to intense stories with psychologically cathartic themes, resulting in scary situations.

As a child, Terrell Newby spent many late-night hours in the back of the classroom and at study groups as his mother pursued a double master's degree in the behavioral sciences at Roosevelt University in Chicago, Illinois. His mother encouraged him as well as his younger brother to understand the relevance of fear as it pertains to the unknown, even with the cultural and social issues.

Terrell Newby attended Columbia College, Chicago, studying communications. Later he attended Argosy University, where he studied psychology, and Purdue University, studying Behavioral Psychology.

The author is a former television news journalist and film producer. He is an Army Airborne Veteran serving as a SOCOM Knight Stalker, Fort Campbell, Kentucky. At 25, he purchased the construction permit to put on the air radio frequency 730am in Madison, Alabama, original call letters WDKT currently WUMP. He is fond of exploring uncharted parallel universes of living beings. He enjoys training his Doberman, playing tennis, and golf. Having once owned a squirrel monkey, he now likes collecting Red Devil fish.

CONTENTS

The Horrors of Inferno

GHOST OF PALMYRA HIGH

CHAPTER 1

Mysteries of the Baffling Black Book

A LOW MOAN FOLLOWED BY A SOFT "OH MY GOD" escapes from his lips as he clenches his chest while his eyes widen, struck with horror. Sliding down the wall at the pace of a snail and wiping what he thought were tears, he realizes something that thoroughly shakes him to the core. Fresh, red blood, instead of tears, were oozing out of his nose and eye tear ducts. Bracing his 6'3" frame body, he manages to reach for the back of the janitor room wall. Sliding down the wall and grabbing his ink pen one final time, he takes notes of this twilight moment of his life.

This is just one unbelievable experience documented in the black composition book that I found a couple of days ago. But before

1

I continue reading and surprise myself with the shocking and partly sickening events shared by the owner of this notebook, I must introduce myself and how I found this journal.

I'm known as Dr. Kneel, a retired, divorced college professor in my late 70s. I used to teach at the University of Nebraska, a retired dean of its history department, with a Ph.D. in history from Yale University and a second Ph.D. in Economic & Social History from the University of Edinburg, United Kingdom.

One late summer afternoon, about a week ago, I was walking my high-stung Doberman, named Chester, near a partially burned home with a 'for sale by owner' sign in front of the house. While I was noticing the house and its debris scattered here and there, Chester pulled so hard on his leash that it instantly came out of my hand.

Within a few seconds, Chester runs into the house. Not willing to go inside the house, I call for him to come out a couple of times. Five minutes later, I hear loud barking and growling. He jumps out through an open bedroom window with a black notebook in his mouth. Chester runs toward me, drops the book, and sits whimpering at me. He barks, then looks at the book as to say, *"Pick it up."* Moments later, he stands up on his two hind legs like a human, barking in my face, and then looking around for a while, he finally directs his focus back on me. His ears pointed toward the bright sunny sky, barking as if he were communicating with something or perhaps someone.

Reluctantly, I pick up the damp book with ashes reeking the smell of smoke and a strange odor of burnt meat but not like human-kind. Chester and I walk a mile and a half back home. After cleaning up and putting on my smoking jacket, I wipe down the book by using my hair blower, drying off the pages gradually.

After taking a shower and putting on my blue cotton robe, I pour myself some merlot wine. Then, I pick my pipe and throw on a few logs on the fire. When I finally sit down with this book that my dog went crazy over, I first inspect it. Initially, I realize that it's nothing more than a typical school-type composition notebook. But on a closer look, I see that it is a bit frail, beat up, and somehow unusual, filled with lots of pages. Inside, I notice several worn-out and some burnt spots, along with a few red splatters throughout the book.

After 30 years in the classroom, I try to live an active yet simple life, away from unnecessary troubles. Little did I know how one day, my ACE Award-winning search and rescue Doberman would find himself caught up in a real-life ghost triangle, bringing himself *and me* several worries. Chester has a typical history of finding children lost in the wilderness, elderly folks wandering from nursing homes, finding lost hikers in the woods. He has been called to rescue during earthquakes, train wrecks, fires, plane crashes and tornadoes, and various other natural disasters. Chester has an ultra-sensitive ability to hear almost any and everything. He manifests great night vision, keen endurance smell, and a two-foot vertical hump from all four paws. He is capable of walking on two hind legs for up to 100 yards in search of his assigned subject. Chester turned out to be, well, let's just say, beyond strange. Even right now, he is sitting attentively like a statue, watching me as I read this fascinating yet bizarre diary of a man who suffers immense physical as well as emotional pain.

Taking a long drag from my pipe, I open the first page of the black composition notebook whose caption reads: *Palmyra high school joys and disappointments*. Midway through my read, I notice the water in my pipes starts moving at an exceptionally higher pace and rattles the tube beyond measure. It starts shaking so loud I think it'll explode any second. I put the book down in an instant and stand up. Chester starts pacing back and forth, going up on his two hind legs, and then jumping up and down, barking. The noise stops. Wow, what the hell. I wipe the sweat off my face and neck, sit back down, refocusing my mind on this insane read. Drinking more wine, I resume reading.

Dating back to his troubled childhood leading to the first day this guy, Biff Saw, was hired by his former high school swim teammate of four years. Janitor Biff worked at Palmyra High School for 30 years. Biff was a 6' 2" tall white male, age 75, with long gray hair, a short white beard with what he describes as a crow-size nose. While in elementary school, he explains in great detail how as a kid, he was teased about his nose to the extent that he decided to join the swim team, thinking by becoming massively fit and athletic, he would become popular. Even though he won numerous awards during his youth for his exceptional swimming skills, in high school, his nose would always become the subject of jokes and teasing. When not swimming, he was a recluse. Unable to keep a girlfriend, he spent most of his time reading books or working out with weights, sometimes swimming and running an extra 20–30 miles a day at the local YMCA.

Biff's parents owned and managed apartments and leased farm properties to cattle and corn farmers. He was an only child, as his parents had lost twin boys only three hours after they were born. Biff's mother became withdrawn from him, showing no affection toward him at age seven. Shortly thereafter, his mom suffered a mild stroke. Biff's dad would tell him his mom was taking medication, suffering from a post-partum psychotic disorder, adding she was depressed over losing his twin brothers.

As Biff gets older, he helps feed his mother, who often sits in a rocking chair, staring out their backyard window. His mom only responds when a picture of the twins in their incubators is pried from her hands for bathing.

Biff carried the lack of affection and his deformed crow-size-nose complex throughout his childhood. After graduating from high school with honors, he joins the United States Navy. Biff then writes about finding a sense of self-worth and how swimming gives him peace of mind and power. He then shares an incident that happened late one night, which goes something like this:

One night, after getting drunk at the naval base bar with a woman he refers to as "Sunshine," they screwed each other's brains out. "Sunshine," a Naval officer, and Biff, enlisted as a sailor, worked in the same military command company. Weeks later, when Biff's "Sunshine" found out that she was pregnant, they decided to get married so that they do not get kicked out of the service.

"Sunshine" Cliff, now Mrs. Saw, a former mass communication specialist, first met Biff on a Naval ship when Biff was 35 while she herself was just 25 years old. After their drunken night at the bar, they get married, and nine months later, she gives birth to triplets—two boys and one girl.

"Sunshine" and Biff, at this point, are 20 years retired from the Navy. Biff writes about his "Sunshine" being the publisher of the town's local newspaper—a popular paper that she inherited from her father and mother. The paper called *The Chronicle* had been in the family since 1901. The original two-story building where the paper was published still stands and is on the National Historical Record downtown. *The Chronicle* is the tallest building in the city. The paper services five neighboring cities. The city has a modest population of 566 residents and is more of a quaint village in Otoe County, Nebraska. Livestock auctions still happen in the community. Moreover, this region has farmers throughout the county.

Unlike his wife, Biff works at a school. In 1990, after retiring from the Navy at the age of 45, he was hired as the chief maintenance supervisor by the school's principal. According to Biff's work attire on the job, he wears a dark blue janitor uniform with his name sewed onto the left side as Biff. He also wears military-style black frame eyeglasses.

Biff describes how toward the latter stages of his Naval career, he began taking medication for hypertension, an early sign of heart disease. Biff has always carried a complex about his wife's affection toward him. His insecurity often led him to accuse her of not really wanting him because of his large nose and noticeable cut under his eye. The retired Navy diver sailor writes that he sustained a notice-able cut mark under his left eye during a bar fight after a guy he was shooting pool with kept mocking the size of his nose.

Going through the notebook, I found out that Biff was offered the position of maintenance supervisor about 30 years ago by his former high school swim team member and friend Luke Peppers, who was also the principal of the high school at the time. Luke and Biff spend many summers weekends fishing for bass and catfish, traveling to lakes in Nebraska, Iowa, Wisconsin, and Michigan.

Throughout the years of Biff's tenure as a janitor, he tells the story of how he was known as the *friendly janitor*, always giving students candies and balloons for getting good grades. Biff had a passion for kids getting an education. While he was still in the Navy, he had acquired a degree in engineering. His wife, on the other hand, carried a master's degree in English.

During his days at the school, he had an understanding with all the honor students and often showered them with gift cards, balloons, and pastries. Biff and his wife would set up an elaborate session in the school gym for fall and spring, enjoying the report card celebrations. In his diary, he then writes about how a group of rogue students decided to crash the celebrations out of nowhere one day, harassing not just the honor students but also Biff and his wife, "Sunshine." They walked into the gym where the celebrations were taking place, ran in different directions, burst balloons, and stole cupcakes and soda. Some of them threw dirt on the gym floor and released mice from the science lab, while others poured honey on the floor, causing some of the students to get stuck on the gym floor or fall and break teeth by busting chins, bleeding on their clothes. They complained unreasonably that the celebrations were not fair and demanded that they too get some of the candies and pastries. Considering their demand to be unfair, Biff tells them that they need to study harder and must earn those treats.

From that day onward, some disgruntled male students begin harassing Biff by putting glue on his janitor door handle and defecating and urinating on the bathroom floors at the end of the school day. Painting in red on some of the bathrooms, a girl used her lipstick on the bathroom mirrors, writing "asshole janitor." On several occasions, the teens found it hilarious rigging up a booby trap in bathrooms, making Biff's mop bucket fall on or in front of him when he opened the bathroom door. They even poked holes in the large trash barrels, so when he lifted the trash out of the container, it spilled on the floor. They enjoyed urinating in soap dispensers and making a mess of everything. This deviant behavior went on for several weeks.

Biff writes about his wife going to the principal and complaining about the nuisances. Since Biff didn't want to bother his friend with the matter at hand, he tries to put an end to it in some other way. Biff's "Sunshine" writes an editorial for the in-town paper with the topic being "Parents and Their Deviant High School Children." In this article, Biff gives a complete account of his confrontations with the group of four to six teens, boys as well as girls, who kept trying to make Biff's job miserable at all cost. He also attempted several times to put an end to the situation by trying to encourage the rogue students to change their behavior or suffer the consequences.

When that didn't help, Biff's wife went so far as to confront some of the parents after school, often threatening to expose their families in her newspaper. Most of the parents found a way to get their teens to end the childish harassment. But four students, three guys and one girl, insisted on perpetual harassment, waiting until nearing the end of school, often leaving from the teachers' exit or simply running into the computer lab after school or sitting in on tutoring sessions.

This cat-and-mouse game between Biff and the teens started a couple of weeks out from the start of the school's spring break. These incidents among some high school students and the janitor escalate in the breezy Nebraska winter-spring transitional season.

One evening when Biff is preparing his janitorial items for work, those three teen boys and the girl throw loud firecrackers in the janitorial closet where he was working. Soon after that, the boys run off down three flights of stairs along with the girl and step outside, laughing uncontrollably. They hop on their bikes, peddling off into the woods.

Meanwhile, startled by the unexpected multi-able banging sounds, Biff tries to turn his body in the direction of the sound but slips on spilled soapy water. As a result, his glasses fall from his face. He grabs his chest, coughing, and tries to get his medication out of his pocket but fails.

Biff investigates the light and slumps over on the floor, dead.

But then, a black, shadowy image of Biff slowly steps outside of his body. The image puts his hand on his hips, shakes his head in disgust, and walks down the long school hallway lined with school lockers, where he finds a black composition notebook. His dark image walks into a classroom, sits down at a student desk, and drops the black notebook down on the wooden desk. The lines on the pages begin filling up, describing in graphic detail his last living minutes prior to his death, this time recording in red blood how he just experienced death from the mischievous acts of three teen boys and one girl.

Oblivious to all of this, "Sunshine" continues to wait for her husband Biff to arrive home. Having just prepared their favorite Friday evening dinner—lamb chops, green beans, salad, catfish from last weekend's fishing trip with his buddy from school—her eyes remain on the door, waiting and anticipating her husband's arrival. Macaroni salad and iced tea continue warming up. Along with the mouth-watering meal, Biff's "Sunshine" prepares a surprise dessert, especially for her husband. She places the muffins back in the oven but forgets to take away the kitchen towel.

After leaving the kitchen, she goes into the family room to watch some television, mainly to kill time. While watching television and waiting for Biff, "Sunshine" falls asleep and completely forgets to turn off the oven. Two hours pass by, and during this time, the house catches fire. There is still no sign of Biff. Neighbors rush into the house and see the kitchen blazing black smoke. Bellowing and coughing with their eyes burning, four of the neighbors crawl on the floor into the dining room, using their clothes to block the black smoke and somehow manage to save "Sunshine" barely.

After being rushed to the hospital and coming to her senses, "Sunshine" is hysterical about where Biff is. She keeps asking if her husband is in the hospital. Around 6 a.m. the next day, that is, on Saturday, neighbors contact "Sunshine's" children, and everyone tries to figure out where Biff is located.

Biff's physical body lies dead from Friday, 5 p.m., until it is discovered early the next morning. It happens when the high school basketball coach comes into the school around 7:30 a.m. to prepare for basketball practice. Unable to find any dust mops to dust the gym floor, the basketball coach takes the elevator to the third floor. But much to his chagrin, the elevator door doesn't open. Frightened, with his heart racing, the coach pushes the third-floor button several times until it cracks, the door finally opens. He walks toward the janitor's closet. When he hears footsteps, he speaks up, "Hey! Who the hell is in here? Whoever you are, you're not supposed to be here after hours. show yourself." Breathing heavily and a bit startled by the mysterious footsteps, the coach slowly walks down the hallway toward the janitor's closet. He looks into a classroom or two, then looks up toward the janitor's closet and sees Biff's body slumped on the floor with his glasses in front of him and eyes bucked.

Soon "Sunshine" gets the devastating news that her home is now unlivable from the accidental fire. She is then told that her husband has passed away as a result of a massive heart attack. After the sad funeral attended by faculty, staff, former swim team members, and several Navy friends, most of the high school students come to pay a visit, except those who technically were responsible for Biff's massive heart attack. Midway through spring break after school, students who were responsible and happened to be graduating in three months sneak back into the school, gather in the science lab, and perform a blood oath. Using a scalpel, each cuts a small slit on their index finger and then press their bloody fingers together, mixing their blood among themselves. They swore to never talk about what happened to janitor Biff for life, promising to take their actions to the grave.

* * *

The professor in me decides to do some research regarding the tragic death of this guy named Biff. I lay the black composition book down, log on to the internet, and start Googling. I find out his wife, a woman named Ariel, who had been cooking dinner on the same Friday night Biff died. That's when I realize that the woman Biff refers to as "Sunshine" throughout the book is actually a woman known as Ariel.

As I continue with my research, I come across several unusual and hard-to-believe events that followed Biff Saw's death. For instance, after he died, the school decides to contract janitor services. Shortly after his death, custodians report hearing strange noises: toilets flushing, rattling water pipes, talking voices in empty classrooms, doors slamming when no one is in school. Several previous custodians reportedly heard a vacuum running in a nearby room, even though they swear it was shut off. Word gets out that there is a wing of the school's third floor that is haunted. There are reports of numerous janitorial replacements. Several janitors literally run out of the building in the middle of their shifts, quitting in tears, with headaches, stomach pains, and permit respiratory problems. Former janitors reported stories of nightmares and needing psychiatric counseling.

A time came when no one wanted to take the job as the school janitor. Undoubtedly enough people concluded these bizarre phenomena were not worth the risk of being horrified and traumatized at work, and maybe there was some truth to the stories and myths circulating around the Palmyra community about the school being haunted, particularly during nights.

While surfing through the internet, I came across several pictures of the burnt house that was now in shambles. There was a newspaper picture of a kitchen fire burning most of the house. I immediately recognized the house as the one Chester went into to get the very diary that I'm reading. *This doesn't make any sense,* I murmur to myself.

While I'm still contemplating the whole situation and going through the events described in this baffling black book over and over again, I feel chills going down my spine. As I try to join the pieces of this complex puzzle in my head, the hair on my arms rise, and my whole-body trembles faintly. I take my glasses off, grab my gray beard, and begin to mentally ponder as to what the hell is going on. My mind is racing a hundred miles per hour as I try to make sense of what is happening to my body. I reach for the book that I had earlier placed on my office study desk, but to my surprise, it's nowhere to be found. I look under every piece of paper in desk drawers and the bookshelves. I walk into my bedroom, living room, dining room, looking everywhere, but find nothing.

At that moment, I hear water running up and down the plumbing in my house; pipes start rattling, toilet bowl tops up and down in my home, flapping loudly. I start sweating uncontrollably. Tears and snot roll down my face, and physical emotions take control. I realize I can't stop my own body. Now I'm literally on the floor, crawling like an infant into a corner in my study. I shake hysterically and grab both shoulders in an attempt to calm myself. But all in vain. My ears ring, my teeth chatter, and I hear one of them crack. Then I bite the side of my tongue, feeling something in my mouth. I spit blood and a small portion of my tongue. "Oh, my God."

The madness stops abruptly as my doorbell rings. I manage to open the door, and Chester dashes out instantly. I call him to come back. He looks back at me while in full stride, then looks forward, running into the woods like lighting.

CHAPTER 2

Alex – The New Janitor

PALMYRA HIGH SCHOOL'S PURSUIT OF FINDING A JANI-tor continues. After looking for the right person for day and night, they finally find Alex, a young 17-year-old high school teenage guy who is willing to work as a janitor.

Coming back from out of town and still studying in high school, Alex is basically looking for a part-time job. After returning, going back to his previous job was out of the question. That's mainly because he had failed to notify his boss before leaving for a trip during the Christmas holidays from December to January. But now, starting back at school, a part of him hopes and wishes to get his earlier job back. After giving it some thought, he heads to his former boss, praying that he succeeds in his mission. Much to his dismay, his old boss gets furious the moment she sees him and instantly asks him to leave, never to show his face again.

Sad and disappointed, Alex begins job-hunting. After getting a referral for an institute from a family member who used to work for the same company that fired Alex, he thinks of giving it a try. He also goes online, signs up for some places, and applies at various companies, but nothing fruitful comes out of his hard work. Although some people do give him calls and ask him to come for an interview, no job description fits Alex's busy schedule. Since he is still studying, he looks for nighttime jobs only, but almost all the places he applies to offer day-time jobs.

Alex's plan was to study in the morning, then go home and relax for a while and then later, at night, go to his job. He continues to search for a place that would be in accordance with his plans. But when he is unable to find such a job, his mother suggests he go try out a place called "working labor ready." She tells him how that place will get him a temporary job but nothing permanent. At this company, one is supposed to fill in for people who are not there or who missed days or are just quitting and get paid for that day only.

After contemplating about the job description, Alex decides to give it a shot. *Anything is better than nothing,* thinks Alex to himself.

The next morning, he goes to the temp agency, signs a few papers, and takes a 100-question exam given by a guy named Jay. Initially, everything went smooth but when Alex was doing the exam questions on his computer, its screen turned black. It was like a computer malfunction because of which Alex was unable to complete the test. Technicians were called to fix the system but for some reason, none of them could repair it.

When they failed to restore it even after several attempts, Jay said, "Alex, looks like you need to come back the next day and take the same test again tomorrow."

"But I was hoping to start working from today only," said Alex with a bit of frustration in his tone.

Seeing that Alex was clearly annoyed by the whole setback, Jay changed his mind, saying, "Well, how about we let it slide this time?" Then after a brief pause, he continued, "You're hired, Alex. I will give you a call in case anything's available. Sounds cool?"

"Absolutely! Thanks!" replied Alex as his cheeks flushed with excitement.

The next day, Alex gets called about some simple cleaning out of offices and a few other handy jobs. These jobs varied in terms of their requirements, but Alex was cool with it, as far as it gets him out of his mom's house. At this point, all that Alex really wants is to look after his two-year-old daughter and provide for her.

However, soon, he realizes that working with a temp agency would not work for him or his daughter in the long run because neither the work nor the income was steady. To look after himself and his daughter, he wanted a permanent job that paid relatively more than his current job. Working with a temp agency meant you might work for two consecutive days and then not work for, say, the next three days or perhaps a week, and this is something that Alex decided to change. For the time being, however, he continued to work with the temp agency.

About a week later, the agency assigned a task to Alex, which he considered was more of an opportunity to him. Basically, it was for two weeks or a week straight. Alex had to work at a Pinnacle Bank Arena in which a place was allotted for concerts, basketball games, monster trucks, and rallies. This seemed to grasp Alex's attention, as it meant work along with entertainment.

There were a lot of games that week, so they needed extra people to come and clean up after the games. Alex, who took the opportunity and agreed to work for a week, was going to receive $500 for his service, which was more than what he was making. Although each shift was eight hours long, he decided he wasn't going to turn the opportunity down.

Once Alex takes up the task, he works from around 11 p.m. to 3 a.m., depending on how bad the area is. On his third day at the Pinnacle Bank Arena, he gets a bit tired, thinking he has to wake up early for school the next morning. Going to sleep around three in the morning and then getting up at 7 a.m. is no easy task. But Alex remains persistent and doesn't give up.

Amongst the group of temp workers hired by the agency, Alex is the youngest. Unlike others, Alex is neither a drug addict nor has past criminal records. He is not like the other workers who are there only because they were unable to keep steady jobs in the past. Some of his co-workers were homeless, not having their own transportations. When Alex saw himself working with such a group of people, he'd often feel bad for himself. However, he is not the only one who feels this gap between himself and his co-workers. Ashley, the temp agency boss who hires only temp workers, notices Alex's good work ethics and behavior too. One early morning, before getting off from work, she comes to the job site. After pulling Alex to the side, she speaks with him about getting an actual job with regular pay and reasonable working hours for a high school student.

Standing near the time clock and after Alex punches out, Ashley asks him several questions about changing jobs. Despite being tired and having an Algebra test the next morning, Alex curiously listens to what Ashley has to say. "Basically, there are two buildings that you could work at." When Alex nods, Ashley continues, "One is a hospital, a simple cleaning job. But there is one problem: it is a bit far away, and the working hours might not match up with your school schedule. But there's another one which I think is better suited for your routine." Then after a brief pause, she said, "It is Palmyra High School. This job is closer to your house and would fit your schedule better. The rest is for you to decide."

After his conversation with Ashley, Alex starts considering working at Palmyra High School. He decides that it is a perfectly good opportunity for a first job.

* * *

After accepting the Palmyra High School janitorial job, Alex exchanges numbers with Ashley. She says she will call him the next day to let him know what time to reach and where to meet the current lady working the evening shift. After connecting with the lady present there who was just covering for the lady who's quitting, Alex is told that he'll be working at the school as the new janitor permanently. Alex is then asked to visit the school by 8 p.m. at night so that he meets her and sees the area of the school and his janitorial duties.

On Monday, after school, Alex rushes to his locker to keep his backpack so that he doesn't get late for his new workplace. Excited and happy, he is in such a hurry that he reaches his new job 20 minutes early. When he sees that the lady he is supposed to meet isn't there, he realizes his mistake. But his excitement doesn't let him feel bad.

While he waits for the lady to arrive, Alex's heart pumps fast, and his hands get a little sweaty. He goes through five or six balls of bubble gum. He must have chewed the flavor from them in two minutes, blowing bubbles, smacking on his gum, loud music playing in his van, just jittery as he waits to work his first real job.

When Alex couldn't sit any longer, he decides to just stand outside the school. Then, 20 minutes later, the lady pulls up. She introduces herself as Samantha. The two exchange their hi and hellos. She then gives Alex a tour of the building, showing him everything that he had to clean, including the desks in the classrooms. There were a couple of clamps back in the classrooms and the hallway, just a few here and there.

The whole job is rather easy, thinks Alex to himself.

The structure of the school was pretty much like a medium-sized school. But it had these two double doors that split down the middle of the school. Basically, it was like one of those high schools that had two doors you could go through. It was during this first visit that Alex noticed something strange. He noticed that when Samantha was showing him around the school, she went super quick. He felt the hairs on the back of his neck move, and then a cold breeze went across his face, touching his lips and face gently and watering his eyes. She showed him, in fact, rushed him through the corridors and talked about what he was supposed to do. Instead of taking four hours to show him around, she took about two and then called it a day.

"Oh, and you got to clean the bathrooms," Samantha added at the end.

After their tour ended, they closed all the double doors, everything. Samantha then showed Alex how to shut all the lights off. It was a weird light outlet that required a special key to shut the lights off. What Alex didn't like about it was that the light switch was by the janitor's closet, and to reach it, one had to walk through a long hallway, immersed in pitch-black darkness. This kind of creeps Alex out, but since he is dedicated to work, he ignores it. After locking all the doors, the two head outside. The lady goes in the car. She offers Alex a smoke (which he accepts) and explains the job further.

While the two were talking, Alex receives a text message on his phone. The message is from Ashley, the CBM boss, asking how things were going. She contacts Samantha too and learns that everything went smoothly. Then she messages Alex again, saying, "Make sure you get the key to the school because the keys opened everything in the school."

Alex considers this to be a little weird considering the fact that he hadn't signed any paperwork or contractual document. Technically, if he'd wanted, he could have done anything with the keys. He could have simply left, disappeared, and never showed back again while having the keys to basically the entire school.

Despite thinking it to be a little odd, Alex asks Samantha to hand him the school keys, to which she readily agrees. "There you go," she says as she throws him the keys and continues, "Good luck, Alex!" After a little conversation with the school principal, Alex says his goodbye and calls it a day.

* * *

The next day, on Tuesday, Ashley wants to come by and show Alex around the school, to which he agrees. The following day, Alex finishes up school, and then around 8 p.m., he reaches the destination but same as before, he arrives a bit early.

The supervisor who had hired him, named Stacey Adams, pulls up 20 minutes later with paperwork that had signed all company-hiring documents with CBM. Stacey proceeds to get him familiar with the school in case the lady he is replacing did not show up that day. He nods his head and agrees to walk through the school. That's when Alex notices that the tone of the supervisor's voice suggested nervousness and fear as her cracking voice said, "Move quickly."

Anyhow, they go into the building, turn on the lights and everything, and are in the first part of the school. Then Stacey says, "You don't have to worry about the front part of the building. It is like the main hall, like the main entrance. But you would, indeed, do some of the front part, especially that has classrooms, in the hallway."

The supervisor then explains to Alex the cleaning duties. When the two walk into the department through the double doors, her mood changes completely. A jolly, carefree woman who had been smiling and laughing so far now turns into an attentive and stiff woman. As soon as they get in the building, her mood goes down to the extent that even Alex feels differently, especially after watching Stacey's face turn pale, almost snow-white, which she doesn't notice. But Alex doesn't say anything. He thinks she might have some disease, and since he didn't want to embarrass her, he doesn't bring the topic up.

Despite that, Alex continues to notice Stacey's changed behavior. He wonders as to why her guard went up in seconds. Nonetheless, he continues to look around the place.

Minutes later, he again notices his supervisor's face and is surprised to see this weird look of fear spread all over her face. Ever since the two began to talk, she would always be in a cheerful mood, joking and laughing around. She'd come as someone who was always in good spirits. But all of that changed the moment they entered the school building.

The more they look around, open the doors and different locks, the more Stacey acts strangely. At one point, Alex swears he heard her teeth click together out of nervousness and is pretty sure that she was sending out silent farts that smelt like sulfur for some reason.

Walking through with Stacey, Alex peeps around, trying to ignore everything, like certain noises that he couldn't tell whether they were coming from the inside or outside of the building. When they go to the far back, she shows him the classrooms, telling him what wastes to throw away. All this was basically told to him by Samantha, who had shown him around the previous day, but Stacey's nervousness was beyond measure. The more she explains, the more uneasiness creeps across her face.

As they keep going and start walking towards the front of the building, Stacey repeats how they clean the areas in the school. Tenseness apparent on her face, she rushes from door to door, trying to get it over with. But when they reach the break room, which is next to the office, Alex feels he can't take it anymore. He feels he needs to ask whether something is bothering her, and without thinking much about it, he says, "Stacey, Is something wrong? You seem a bit distracted. Are you worried about something? You can be honest with me, you know."

"What? Me? Worried?" Then after a brief tensed laugh, she continues, "There is nothing. Everything is fine."

Despite knowing that she is lying, Alex says, "All right, if you say so. But hey, let me know if anything upsets you, okay?"

"Sure, will do," replies Stacey, trying to brush off her fears.

The two continue walking to the break room. As they walk towards it, Alex again senses a weird, concerned look on Stacey's face. He stops and feels he can't take it any longer, then turning to Stacey, he says, "Listen, what's wrong? It feels like something is not right in here, but you're trying to hide it from me." He then continues, "I know the place seems creepy but trust me, I'm not afraid. I just need to work. I'm good. Nothing you say is going to change my mind. So please, tell me what is bothering you."

That's when she starts tearing up and rubbing her hands together. Both could feel the temperature drop to nearly 30-degrees in the room. Alex could not believe his supervisor was wiping tears from her eyes. Then she starts spilling the beans. "This school is haunted," she says nervously. Alex agrees with her, just to encourage her to talk more about the building and its weirdness.

"Honestly, the reason why I didn't want you to know this was because I didn't want to scare you off. A lot of employees in the past have already quit working here." When she sees Alex nodding, she continues, "A female employee hired as a janitor got so scared once that everyone freaked out. Thinking that someone else was in the building, they locked themselves in the room and called 911. Instead of calling me, they called 911. The woman janitor says to the 911 dispatcher to come get her because she is in fear, crying and screaming, thinking there was someone in the building or perhaps someone following her. Similar incidents were reported afterward with the employees saying that the school is creepy."

"Do you trust all of this?" Alex inquired after a while.

"I do not deny that people have had some weird experiences here. Multiple times people call asking us to come and get them out of the building because they feel trapped. Or they feel like there is someone in the building with them. At first, all this sounded funny. I would even laugh at their tiny tales, but then, it's kind of got creepier," replied Stacey.

"Creepier? How so?" asked Alex.

"For example, there was this one lady who told us her stuff got moved, like physically. She also said that she saw shadows and heard weird noises, sounds like people are whispering and talking to her," replied the supervisor.

The two continue to talk. Alex finds out that about four or five employees have had similar incidents. Because of these setbacks, they basically decide to stop working here and quit on the spot. Alex was perhaps the sixth person to work there as the janitor. Seeing the concern on his face, Stacey then says, "I know this is last-minute, and I wasn't even sure about giving you the job only because I didn't want to freak you out. But if I don't get you to go there, it's going to be the other lady. She is filling in for the other lady who left, but she could only be there so long, which is why I hurried up and picked you as a replacement." Then with a frail smile, she continues, "I didn't want to go with another option of finding a replacement. Hope you understand?"

Alex sees the look of fear on Stacey's face and how she was struggling to hide it. It was as if she was anticipating an attack from someone and just wanted to be on guard to counteract in case something was to happen. Although Alex finds it all creepy, he just laughs it off and shows Stacey a not-so-confident 'thumbs up.'

Alex continues to fool himself into believing that he does not believe in ghosts or spirits and shadows. He keeps brushing off such thoughts aside. But a point comes when he too begins to doubt his decision of agreeing to work at a place that is known for being haunted. Rumors around the village are this school has a long history of paranormal activity coming from the third floor of this building. The school was built in the mid-1900s and has a long history of terror.

While Alex stands contemplating about the situation and hearing Stacey talk about more details regarding what happened to the other people, his heart starts beating faster, and the palms of his hands become sweatier than what he's accustomed to. While talking with Stacey and standing in the break room, Alex looks around and sees something that completely shakes him. A black smiley face appears on the whiteboard present behind him. As he turns and sees it, he notices that the face seems to smile, then frown right before their eyes. As his supervisor speaks to him, the tension gets stronger, and the air feels thicker. Alex and Stacey are both equally freaked out. At first, they pretend as if they didn't see what they knew they saw on the whiteboard. But unable to contain the suspense of what was obvious, Alex asks his supervisor, "Did you see that too? Or did my brain process an illusion or what?"

Stacey places her index finger over her red lips, nods her head up and down, confirming, signaling Alex to walk into the next room. Their walk was creepy because it seemed as though they were walking in slow motion. Alex thinks they'll never get out to the classroom.

Alex feels a little adrenaline rush, kind of thrilling. "Even though I don't believe in ghosts," said Alex, "I must say that was really weird." After a brief pause, he continues, "Or maybe it isn't

Stacey, maybe our minds are playing these tricks. You know what, it's better that we just ignore it."

Just as he finishes saying this, Stacey points at certain areas where they could hear pipes moving in the building. That's when Alex starts to freak out, but Stacey somehow tries to stay professional, maintaining a cool demeanor. Every now and then, the two just look at each other with a 'oh well' or 'whatever' expression, pretending what they may have thought they saw or heard was just an older building needing repair. Then they continue walking out of the break room into a small office.

Alex feels relieved as he comes out of that large creepy area. As they walk and look in the direction of the small office across from the break room, Alex notices that the blinds are shut. When he walks into the office with his supervisor, she turns on the small office light switch. Surprisingly, the blinds of the small office room are open wide, which completely catches Alex's attention. He remembers explicitly that when he saw the office from a distance, its blinds were shut but now, standing inside the room, he saw that they were wide open. Alex, however, was not the only one who notices this change. His supervisor, Stacey, is surprised by the blinds too. Her nervousness increases as she looks here and there, trying to get done with her job. She hurries up and is rattled to finish the walk-through. They were both thinking and talking about ghosts just moments ago, and now this happened. They begin to think that perhaps their minds are getting dizzy, and they are simply seeing and sensing things that aren't happening in reality. However, the changes were too obvious to ignore. With anxiousness and fear creeping over the two souls, they finally finished the walk-through.

They walk out toward double doors that weren't there when they first walked into the room. This, again, gets Alex's attention. But then he realizes that perhaps he didn't notice them the first time they entered, as back then, he was concerned about Stacey's behavior and her paranoia.

Stacey then mentions, "That's the back room, back area is between these double doors." Clearing her throat, she continues, "Get this area done first before it gets dark, then shut them and lock the doors."

"Got it," responds Alex reassuringly, "I will be fine."

"Also," she then says, "it might make you feel better being here, in front than being at the back, over there. It's a minor thing just to make yourself feel better."

"I agree," replies Alex.

Once again, they had to shut off that long hallway light after they shut the little double doors. The hallway undoubtedly had a very creepy air to it.

As both Alex and Stacey walk down the hallway, neither one of them looks back or to the side of the hallway. Strange sounds of pipes continue several times, and it seems as if water was running through the wall. It was all spine-chilling for Alex, and he was kind of scared, but by now, his supervisor was trying to play it off cool, and he couldn't let her see him lose his composure; that would be too much for his fragile masculinity to handle.

After taking a quick look at the last room—the male restroom—they both walk outside. A swift, fresh breeze gently touches their faces as they take a sigh of relief. Being done with the walk-through of the Palmyra High, it was now decision time for Alex.

"Alex, I know that this job is a little weird and the building is just too old, but I would recommend you to work as fast as you can. Don't stay back too late in the night. This would be good for you as well as your studies, as you would have to get ready for your school the following day," she continues with a smile, "I hope I do not sound like your mother."

"You kind of do, actually. But, I assure you, I'll give this job my 100 per cent," said Alex.

Alex, at this point in life, is only concerned with the well-being of his two-year-old daughter. He aspires to do everything for her. He is ready to face all the hurdles and all the challenges just for the sake of her little daughter. If becoming responsible at such an early age was needed out of him, he was ready to accept it. While he is thinking of all this, Stacey speaks up, "So, shall we go in the car, do a little interview and then proceed with all the necessary paperwork?"

"Absolutely," replies Alex, hopefully.

Alex signs the contractual agreement and is automatically hired. It was basically the quickest interview that he had ever done in his lifetime. That too in front of the school, in Stacey's car, and not in a typical company office, which Alex thought was kind of weird.

Anyway, once Alex is officially hired, he gets out of her car. Before saying goodbye, she says, "Contact me if you need anything or if you get too scared, just call me or call somebody, and we'll come get you."

"Thanks. But I'm sure I'll be okay," replies Alex.

The two then part their ways and head to their respective homes.

CHAPTER 3

The Battle

THE NEXT DAY COMES, AND ALEX GOES TO HIS SCHOOL, jamming to his radio. He feels a little nervous about his conversation with his supervisor the night before, and all that lady talked about during his walk-through at Palmyra High. He just couldn't stop thinking about it.

In an attempt to refresh his mind, Alex starts vaping as he's driving to class. Choking and coughing, he sprays cologne and gargles with mouthwash after parking his car. After deciding just to brush it off and man up, he gets off from school and picks up his daughter from his school's daycare. He then grabs something to eat from a fast food drive-through and heads home.

While Alex's mom takes care of his daughter, he tries to do some homework. Then, he heads off to his new janitorial job.

Day 1 on the job...

It's still sunny outside as Alex heads out a little early, driving to work. He reaches around 8 a.m., his first time in the school building all by himself. Initially, he feels somewhat uneasy but then puts his shoulders back and murmurs, *What the hell,* and opens the door, walking inside to his new job. He decides to stay focused, get the work done fast, and get the hell out before too late. Once inside this creepy building, Alex locks it and turns on the LED lights even though one can witness the setting sun's thin rays shine into the building through cracks. ‹ 8am ›

Going to the backroom, which is basically part of the school, Alex notices that for some reason, there aren't any windows. There are literally no windows in this entire freaking area. Neither in the office nor in the classrooms.

"Man! I wish there were some windows in this area," whispers Alex.

Alex begins to start collecting trash scattered here and there and puts it in the bin. Then he starts clearing up the other mess. But during all this time, he stays vigilant. He doesn't even put on his headphones and remains alert throughout his shift. While doing the chores, he keeps thinking about all the ghost stories associated with this school.

"Keep working," says Alex to himself as he starts hearing metal water pipes and rattling sounds of moving chairs and then footsteps. Alex stops for a second, but then the sounds stop too. As he resumes, so does the sound. "I just started working here, and this building is tripping on me, really," Alex murmurs to himself.

Alex adjusts his mind and tells himself that there must be kids from this school trying to play tricks on him. Ignoring the thoughts, he heads to the janitor's closet and starts preparing his mop bucket, filling it up to the water level and pouring in floor-cleaning chemicals. That's when he hears a toilet flush, and his earlier suspicion of some kids being in the school further gets endorsed.

Alex then takes out his car keys and places them in the top compartment of his cleaning cart along with his janitor keys. Then he walks toward the girls' bathroom, opens it, and puts the brown rubber door stopper in place. The door remains propped open as Alex starts cleaning the toilets. As he changes paper towels, cleans the mirror, and sinks, he feels as if someone is watching him. When he looks toward the door, he doesn't see anyone standing. Relieved, he continues wiping the sinks, but then he stops again and looks at the bathroom door entrance. This time the hairs on both his arms stand up. He looks toward the right side, but nothing was there. "This is all in my head," says Alex to himself.

Once Alex finishes mopping the bathrooms, he pulls the trash, dumps it outside, and comes back in. He then rings out his mop, puts away his cleaning materials in the janitor's closet, quickly flips all the light switches. Walking backward, not letting a dark room hit his backside, he quickly surveys and analyzes the area, flipping light switches off (which was held mandatory by the school), otherwise Lord knows one might end up leaving them all on. At this point, Alex seems to be freaking out minute by minute. Even though the noises stop and the building has nothing going on—in fact, it's so quiet you can hear a pin drop—Alex is still kind of feeling strange. He feels this weird presence around him.

After closing the double doors, he feels a little better about being in this building alone. At this point, he just knows that he wants to get the rest of the building done as fast as possible. All things considered, it went smoothly for the first day. Although hearing some noises here and there did freak him out to some extent, on the whole, and to his relief, it wasn't terrible.

Day 2

Alex comes in the next day, feeling more secure and confident. His second day cleaning Palmyra High School turns out to be considerably good.

"All I must do is turn that one light on," he murmurs to himself.

It is pitch-black outside. But even if it were sunny, he wouldn't have known, as there were no windows. The only windows that were present were on the way outside of the hallway, and even those weren't large enough to bring in good sunlight, barely enough to really make a noticeable difference in the rooms Alex was cleaning.

As Alex moves from room to room, vacuuming the teachers' lounge, he feels a cold breeze move across his face. He jumps and turns around, feeling as though someone is behind his body. He slowly walks, feeling this presence mirroring every move of his as he then tiptoes out of the room. Although Alex doesn't touch the light switch, it flickers on and off on its own. He begins to freak out as he knows there is no one in the building except for himself.

Alex really tries hard to reverse his thought process, reminding himself constantly that all this is just in his head. "I'm just overthinking everything," says Alex in an attempt to calm his nerves.

Despite experiencing an eerie presence around him, Alex concludes that none of it was a big deal. The rest of his shift goes smoothly. As he drives home, he tries to rid his mind of all the negative thoughts or drama that may have occurred.

"Stay positive, Alex, think positive," he murmurs.

At that moment, Alex realizes that the next day is Thursday, one more day before his spring break starts. He then begins to make plans in his mind. He thinks of going fishing and hanging out at the lake with his friends and a few girls. The whole prospect looks promising, and Alex just can't wait.

Day 3

The next day, after dropping his daughter off with his mom, Alex drives to work. Throughout his ride, he tries to figure out how to get the building done faster while in school so that it gives him more time to spend with his daughter, finish his homework, and get some time with his friends instead of cleaning offices all night. Alex, who usually gets done with his work around 9:15 p.m., depending on how dirty the school is, plans on working faster than usual.

Thinking these thoughts, Alex reaches his workplace. He walks in and, of course, sees that the freaking lights are off. He turns on the lights, goes to the back area, and gets some double doors propped open. He walks towards the back of the school. Today, he thinks of cleaning up the back first, a way of staying closer to the exit, basically. Having his commercial style trash can on wheels called a bruit, his vacuum strapped to his back, and his cleaning spray, toilet cleaner, and janitor rags, he decides to start working from the very last room in the back.

After walking up to the first classroom, he opens the door, looks up, down, and around the classroom and then the teacher's desk. Looking at the large classroom's flat-screen television, he blinks his eyes. Then squinting, he sees a reflection or an image of a person standing inside the television against a dark background. After a quick glance at the power cord dangling from the back of the mounted television, Alex sees that clearly the television is not on. However, he sees a full-grown adult person; it looks like a man's shadow but more like a real image on the unplugged television screen.

Alex quickly rushes to the light switch and flips it on, the adrenaline surging through his body. He tries to make sense of the situation, unable to believe his own eyes.

What the hell is this? Am I really seeing this? This can't be real, thinks Alex as his heart beats rapidly.

Then Alex closes his eyes, and when he opens them, nothing is there. He keeps telling himself not to believe in apparitions, as no such thing exists. But all the while, his legs keep shaking so much so that his knees uncontrollably start trembling and knock knee to knee. They would not stop being shaky, even for a minute.

Grabbing his face and telling himself that he was okay, he calms down and gets it together to some extent. "Stop freaking out, Alex, and get back to work," he attempts to encourage himself.

Alex finishes cleaning up the room, dumping trash, and vacuuming one portion. He then starts cleaning more classrooms in the back area of the school. He walks away, flipping on all classroom light switches, and heads to the closet to get the vacuum. That's when an idea occurs to him. He props open the generator closet with the door kickstand, and as the door stays open, he easily walks back and forth multiple times, cleaning the rooms with no obstructions whatsoever.

When Alex walks back into the classroom to plug his long yellow extension cord for his vacuum, he notices that all the sockets are taken. Only one plug near the teacher's desk is available. Not wanting to interfere with any furniture movement, Alex decides to plug his cord in the hallway socket. Then he starts vacuuming, and everything remains cool for a while. But then, the vacuum stops. When Alex looks at the socket, the cord is on the floor.

Alex walks over, plugs it back in the wall, and starts vacuuming once again. He finishes one area, but as he moves toward the other, the vacuum shuts off. Alex looks over only to find out that the cord is out of the wall again. This is a 20-foot cord, and the area Alex is vacuuming gives him 10 feet of slack. He plugs it in again, but this time, as he's vacuuming, he quickly turns his head, then he just vacuums facing the socket.

After about five seconds, he watches the plug come out of the socket as if an invisible hand took it from the wall, dropping it on the floor. Alex tells himself to stay focused and get the work done, so ignoring everything, Alex keeps working. He goes into the next classroom, and then "Bang," a loud sound comes from nowhere. Alex falls on the floor, scared and shaking uncontrollably. He almost pees in his pants and stays frozen on the floor, listening for the next sound of footsteps or perhaps some other thud. Then he hears it again, "Bang!" It sounds like a door or several doors are slamming.

This catches Alex's attention. He feels these sounds are coming from a far distance. *Maybe a teacher came to pick up some assignments or is preparing for tomorrow. Maybe I'm not the only one in the building,* thinks Alex to himself.

Alex trips hard then and is totally terrified. But after mustering up some courage, he jumps up from the floor, grabs a broomstick. He then realizes he must pee and then figure out what's going on in this school.

Walking fast, now skipping to the nearest bathroom jumping up and down, Alex unzips his pants, and as he pees, he hears another banging sound. He zips up, grabs his broomstick. Peeping around the corner and getting close to the double doors, remembering double doors are next to the janitor's closet—the area where the noise was coming from earlier—Alex steps out.

As he gets closer to the janitor's closet, a pungent smell hits his nose. It's an awful smell like animal feces and urine combined. Alex puts his hand over his nose, choking, coughing, and eyes getting runny. As he peeps around the corner toward the janitor's closet, he sees the door is closed. Hesitant to open it since he had propped it up with the door kickstand, Alex quickly opens the door. There stands a pink baby pig in its urine and defecation with urine running onto Alex's work boots. He closes the door shut and starts running out of the building, determined to kiss this freaky job goodbye.

When he touches the door, he realizes it's locked. *Need to run back to the janitor's closet to get my car keys,* Alex thinks instantly. He turns the corner toward the janitor's closet, and sees the door is wide open with the kickstand holding it, no pig, no shit, no pee, like nothing was ever there. Despite being scared, Alex determines to finish working and decides on cutting back on weed vaping.

Alex stays focused. When he walks back to his work area, he hears his vacuum running. "What the hell," murmurs Alex. He goes into the room, but the vacuum is not running. It was just where he had left it. He finishes the room and dumps the trash.

When he goes to the bathroom, he sees that the door is closed. The lights that he had earlier turned on are now off. He cleans the bathroom, tripping but staying focused.

While getting his tasks done one by one, Alex concludes the place may be haunted and feels he need to not get high before coming to his job. He's totally paranoid in this school yet does his job. He keeps hearing noises, bathroom door closing, toilets flushing, and not that there were any automatic flushers in this school; it's pretty much old with timeworn school toilets and sinks.

As Alex makes his rounds, cleaning and dusting, he keeps feeling a presence that occasionally makes the hair on the back of his neck stand up and his flesh crawl. There is no denying the feeling of some kind of life-like presence is in this school. Although Alex is not as scared, damn he feels anxious. In certain rooms or sections that he walks in, he feels like someone is staring at him.

I just need to confirm because if I do, I'm just going to either confront whatever it is or just totally ignore the thing but I'm not quitting, decides Alex. He feels he'll deal with whatever it is for himself and for his little sweetheart daughter.

Alex starts to slowly understand why so many other janitors quit. This shift is undoubtedly freaky and strange for many reasons. Although he still doesn't believe in ghosts, it's hard for him to ignore this creepiness. As he's playing all these thoughts in his head, he hears another vacuum come on in a room, the one he cleaned about an hour ago. *I'm coming clean and sober to work tomorrow,* Alex decides.

Then on his way to put his cleaning materials back in the janitor's closet, Alex hears doors closing, toilets flushing. Every so often, when he stops walking, the sounds stop too. Even though all of this is freaky, Alex does his best to stay cool. His heart jumps, and the body stiffens as he tries to get used to all the weird happenings, but it is extremely stressful. He hopes to have a better day the following day.

Walking out of the building is always a trip for Alex because he has to turn all the lights off in the building and leave this scary place. He starts turning them off one by one, griping his keys in his left hand, switching off the lights with his left hand. Walking down the long hallway, turning off lights, and walking backward, his back faces the lit areas while his face watches the rooms go dark. Walking backward, he starts hearing keys jiggling and realizes they weren't his. The sound is just above his head. He stops, and oddly, the sound of the keys moving stops too. He resumes walking, holding his own keys so hard his hand starts bleeding. Looking at his hand and still hearing keys jingling, Alex leaves with two lights still on and sprints up the hallway out of the building, locking the door and calling it a freaking night.

Day 4

It's Friday, the start of Alex's high school spring break. With the weekend coming up, Alex plans that as soon as he gets off from work, he will meet his friends and go party, fishing, and camping with his crew. He decides to save the weed smoking and vaping for the weekend. So, his plan is to spot clean and get out of the school well before sundown.

Alex rolls up to clean the school, jamming his radio and feeling good. He is ready to knock out this work and go party later. He gets in with a smile on his face in good spirits. Ignoring the past experiences, he only focuses on doing his job and doing it quickly. He walks to the backroom, turning every light on in the building and getting right to work. He puts his headphones on, listening to some music to make sure he doesn't experience what he did the night before in that very place. He keeps moving about cleaning with headphones on, but his body still feels a presence following him. However, Alex stays focused.

Alex keeps hearing things, sounds like flip footsteps. Some of the classrooms that he walks in to clean turn ice cold but still determined to get out of there soon, Alex remains persistent. He sticks to his routine, moving with precaution to get out early.

Alex then takes out his cell phone to set the alarm to go off thirty minutes earlier than he usually finishes working. But when he looks at the mobile screen, he sees a weather alert pop up on his app, reading of incoming thunder and storm, heading for the Palmyra community. "Heaving storms high wind gust, golf ball size hail expected," says the weather alert. Taking a mental note, he continues hurriedly, trying to spot-clean throughout the school as soon as possible.

When Alex reaches the next room, the teachers' lounge, he realizes that this room too does not have any windows. As he opens the door and steps inside, a thick foggy smoke hits him. It is so cold inside that when he tries to turn on the light, he notices that the switch was iced. Alex steps back, amazed, watching the fog roll over his body.

Before he knows it, he slams the door so hard it shatters the glass portion of the door. When the door shuts, the fog stops simultaneously, and the lights in the room flicker once, then stay on. As Alex sweeps up the glass, he ignores what happened and continues vacuuming the room, cleaning as usual. But he could not help feeling a cold presence in the room.

Something is without a doubt staring at me, he thinks to himself. Alex knows it to be true since he did not vape or smoke weed before coming to work that day. His back is to the teachers' desk, and the presence he feels is also at his back.

Alex, although aware of a presence around him, continues to keep cleaning the entire time. All he wants, at his point, is to get done with his work and leave before the storm hits. So, he continues his work ignoring the eerie coldness in the place.

By the time he is almost done in the backroom, the sound of a loud pop and heavy cracking clamor rumbles through his body. It begins raining heavily on the building. This is exactly what Alex was hoping to avoid. Heavy banging sounds of white rocks pounding the school rooftop could be heard clearly.

Alex walks to the double doors where his cleaning cart is parked. As he opens the double doors near the janitor's closet, a white light flashes outside the next classroom that he is about to clean. It brightens the whole room, and through the corner of his eye, Alex sees a tall man dressed in a janitor's uniform with a dark frame coke-bottle thick lenses, smiling at him. "Oh shit," escapes Alex's mouth as he tries to make sense of the situation.

Alex tries to run, but his body refuses to move. The whole scene looks like a dream or perhaps a slow-motion picture. Alex continues to scream as sweat drips from his forehead. He is so scared that he starts crying right there on the spot. He tries to gather up his courage and runs in the middle of the hallway, breathing heavily now and totally tripping. That's when lightning strikes the building, and all the lights go out, the school submerges in complete darkness.

Alex hates the dark. His first instinct is to grab his car keys and bounce out of this place. But the moment he starts to leave, the electricity is restored. As he runs, while eyeing his cleaning cart that has the two sets of keys—one to open and close the building and the other his car keys—his heart races faster than normal. He's so frightened and sweating so much his shirt gets wet and his hair drips sweat in his eyes. This run toward the cart feels like he's running on a sandy beach. *Will I ever get to this freaking cart, man!* thinks Alex furiously. At that moment, lightning strikes a powerline outside, creating sparks because of which the lights of the building go off again.

The lights then start flickering on and off as if something or perhaps someone is standing at the main breaker box in the building, playing with the building's lights. They just keep fluctuating really bad and making a loud, buzzing noise. As Alex is about to grab his keys, the main door starts shaking, and he hears a loud door-lock sound echo throughout the building. Without further ado, he grabs his keys and runs toward the doors. They start shaking just as he's trying to open them up. They continue to shake but still do not open for Alex. He keeps pulling the handle of the door as lights continue to flicker. He falls backward, still pulling the doors.

As a result of pushing and pulling the doors, they finally fling wide open. Running to his car, Alex finally feels relieved. The pouring rain and lightning felt comforting and reassuring to Alex in comparison with the terror of the school. As he opens the car and sits inside, soaking wet, coughing, wiping his face and breathing heavily, Alex screams out of frustration. Clinching his fists, he screams several times hysterically. Reaching in his pocket, he grabs the keys to start his car and spin away from that crazy place.

As Alex tries to put the key in the ignition, panic sets in as he realizes that he has grabbed the wrong keys from his janitor cart. "Damn it! No, no, no!" screams Alex nonstop. Hail thrashing on his car, he pounds the steering wheel of his car in exasperation, lightning flashing outside the car. He looks back at the school and sees that the lights are completely off. No power means no car keys.

He then thinks of just walking 30 miles home in the storm and then come back later to get his car or just call one of his friends. But then he realizes that his car was the only means of transportation for his spring-break weekend party. *I would have just called for a pickup or Uber, but my car is needed for the partying,* ponders Alex. *None of my dudes has their own car, and I know their parents are not going to let them spend the weekend with their cars at some campground.*

After contemplating the situation for a few minutes, Alex decides to call his best friend D'Angelo, also his high school classmate. They both often hung out after school, vaping and smoking blunts. Plus, he always had good party stuff. *I've got to call my dude,* thinks Alex.

Just as he is about to give his friend a call, he thinks it to be kind of embarrassing. To call someone to help Alex get his keys from inside his workplace would be humiliating. *Whoever I call is going to think I'm a punk, too chicken to go back inside a dark building using my cell phone light to simply get my freaking car keys,* reflects Alex.

Sitting in his car, Alex thinks he can do it himself. But he is also aware of the terror associated with the school building. Going inside in the dark without a backup was out of the question. So, he calls his pal D'Angelo and convinces him to meet him in the school parking lot for $100. He was still tripping but agreed, believing Alex's excuse of needing more light as it was such a big building. D'Angelo informs Alex that he'll be bringing their classmate Amelio. "The more cell lights, the better it is," says D'Angelo.

Thirty minutes later, about 11 p.m., his dudes pull up. Alex sees that everybody is ready for the spring break party. So much so that they take the booze, food, ice coolers and put them in Alex's car before they go into the school. D'Angelo then says, "Hey listen, my sister is going to have someone drop her off here, at the school, to get my parents' car later in the night. Cool?"

"Yeah, sure, brother," replies Alex in a rush.

After saying this, the three walks into the dark building with drizzle dropping on their heads. Alex reminds them that this will be quick, "Just need to grab my keys, and then we're off to party."

"The keys are on the second floor," Alex tells them as they walk into the building with confidence, not a single scared bone in their bodies. Walking down the hallway, it starts getting darker. They turn on their cell lights.

"Dam ya'll, I don't know about ya'll but it's getting colder," speaks up Amelio, "smells gross in here, like an old person's house, and it's starting to get creepy."

"Alex, dude, hope your keys are in your cart cause I'm about to turn around and hall ass," says D'Angelo. The three slowly walk up the stairs, down a short hallway, then to the second hallway. The building is unusually very quiet.

They reach that long hallway that Alex hates walking down. *Oh, my goodness, it's just so freaking creepy,* thinks Alex, but remains silent. For some reason, he always needs to pee badly down this hallway, but there is no bathroom in sight. At that moment, D'Angelo shines the light right at Alex's supply cart.

"I see it. I can take off for my keys," says Alex.

"Dude, you look scared, like your complexion is almost pale white. What's up in this place? I know it's scary as a MOFO. Whatever let's get these keys and get the hell out of here, Alex," says D'Angelo.

"Guys, walk with me to the cart," replies Alex, swallowing hard, admitting he was tripping but would feel better if his friends had his back since they all agreed that the building was creepy.

They walked toward the cart as Alex tries very hard to keep it together. But just as he reaches for his car keys, he notices that they are not there. Alex shakes the cart, looking everywhere, with a bewildered look on his face.

"Dude, what's up? You can't find your key? You don't know where they are?" asks Amelio.

Alex turns around, looks at them to say something, but seconds later, his cleaning cart lifts ten feet off the ground into the air. It stops mid-air, flies through the air, slamming violently against the hallway walls, and shatters into thousands of tiny plastic pieces. It's an "oh shit moment" for the three boys.

All the doors in the school start shaking. The lights in the building start fluctuating and flickering like a strobe light in a nightclub. There's no explanation for this...

Aurelio - 16 - One of the "Gang of 4", the 4 high school student responsible for killy Beff's death . The least intelligent one of the group + the most hapless + very naive, First kidnapped victim of the ghost

MARTHA - 17 - Aurelio's girlfriend one of the gang of 4 - daddy's girl

Jason, pg 72
Brandon

Jane,
Crystal - 9F - nosey .

Mama's Store

ALEX IS AT A COMPLETE LOSS FOR WORDS. HIS HANDS tremble, and his throat dries up as he feels like falling on his knees, crying and screaming his lungs out. He had absolutely been confident about his keys being in his cleaning cart next to the generator keys; it was a part of his nightly routine.

After making an attempt to calm his nerves, Alex turns around and says to his friends, "Dudes, do not panic. Let's search the desks in the school's classrooms."

"But this is cutting into the party time, dude," complains D'Angelo, irritated. "Let's make it quick." Then after a brief pause, he continues, "Or how about we just leave the keys, and come back Sunday night?"

"No, let's look for them one more time, quickly," replies Alex, laying great stress on the last word.

Hearing the annoyance in Alex's voice, D'Angelo doesn't argue back. Amelio, together with D'Angelo, starts walking ahead of Alex, looking for the keys. Alex nervously walks behind them, praying under his breath that they find the keys without wasting much time.

While searching for the lost item, Alex once looks at his cell phone and sees that it's almost 1 a.m. "I have never been here this late before," thinks Alex.

The building is quiet. The three boys continue walking, shining lights all over the place, opening different doors of the school, going in and out of classrooms, the teachers' lounge, and bathrooms. When the three meet in the large hallway, a cold draft and fog ooze through the school walls and beneath their feet. Bewildered, the three friends look around and then at each other. As they try to take off, they realize that they are frozen in their places. They attempt to pick up their feet, but underneath there is a vomit-color sticky substance.

The boys hear the wind whistling through the room. "What is that sound? I am hearing it for the first time inside the building," says Alex. Still stuck in their respective places, the fog in the hallway becomes so thick that they can no longer see each other, and that's when they hear heavy footsteps. It sounds like a giant is walking to the sound of keys jingling.

Alex, D'Angelo, and Amelio begin screaming at once. They try to call for help but can't hear themselves. Suddenly the fog stops, and the three screaming boys stand facing each other, going completely silent.

"Dam ya'll, are we in some kind of messed up dream? If so, it needs to end right now!" says D'Angelo nervously.

"Alex, dude, we got to bounce, get out of this crazy school. We need to get to the camp, smoke a blunt, drink, girls, all that man! Forget the keys, call a locksmith. I'll see you guys outside," says Amelio as he begins to walk off.

With that, Alex and D'Angelo decide to follow Amelio too. They try walking, moving slowly because of the sticky vomit-like substance on the bottom of their shoes. The gooey substance keeps them from walking fast but they try their best to keep their balance, walking and practically sliding on the floors.

Then they take off their shoes and start running toward the double door to get out. They hear the double doors shutting. *Not a good sign,* thinks Alex, *these are the only two doors between the first and second half of the school's exit.* Brushing aside his thoughts, Alex keeps moving forward. They keep running, looking at each other with fear and panic etched on their faces. As the door shuts, they hear a loud bang and an ear-piercing lock sound. *This ain't good, it's all bad now,* thinks Alex to himself.

Realizing the front entrance is not going to be a realistic place to exit, they stop running. They're nearly out of breath, bending over, holding their knees, and sweating their asses off. Panting heavily, Alex says, "Guys, look, I know some emergency exits we can try." They look around the corner and follow Alex to the first emergency exit, but find it locked. Then the three boys throw a large metal object at the glass portion of the door, which bounces off back toward them like a rubber ball. Disappointed and panicked, the boys take off for a second exit door, but it doesn't open up either. They throw several hard objects at the glass portion of the emergency exit door, but to their surprise, everything bounces off back in their direction.

After the same thing happens at the third exit, they completely flip out. Alex's friends start cussing at him, blaming him for getting them caught up in that nightmare from hell. Alex feels terrible about the whole situation but still manages to remain optimistic. *We can still get to our spring break party,* feels Alex. The boys sit in the middle of the hallway in a circle, their hands on their knees, breathing heavily from the frantic back and forth exit runs.

Feeling trapped, they still mentally search for alternative exit ideas. While they whisper out their thoughts back and forth, in the background, they hear multiple sounds of keys jingling, echoing throughout the school. They try listening for the direction from where the sound comes, but it is impossible as the sound has a three-way ricochet effect within the school walls.

At that moment, a large male shadow appears on the ceiling, going toward the boys. When they see it, they jump up, running down the hallway toward the school stairs, which take them up to the second level. On their way up the stairs, several yellow janitorial mop buckets start rolling down the stairs in the direction of the boys, splashing piping hot water from them. The water burns their skin. D'Angelo is hit in the head by the wheel of a bucket, knocking him to the floor onto the hot water.

"Oh shit, oh shit, help me! The water is burning my skin!" says D'Angelo, whimpering hysterically. Slipping up and down the stairs, Alex and Amelio manage to crawl their way down toward the bottom of the stairs, helping D'Angelo out of the water and drying him off with bathroom towels. On their knees and helping, they feel a cold presence, along with the sound of keys jingling getting closer. Although the shadow is over their bodies, there is no physical presence whatsoever. But then the shadow attacks them, chasing the three boys speedily.

Unable to grasp the weirdness of the situation, the boys start running away from the shadow. That's when this eerie thing tries to tackle them. Showing his power with a physical presence, he grips Alex's leg. Alex sees the shadow's full figure and feels his large hand trying to pull Alex toward him. But Alex doesn't let him win this time. He pulls hard, leaving the shadow his sock.

The boys run, ducking and dodging all over the school, determined to outpace and beat this freak. They see light at the end of a hallway and dash for their lives toward the light shining at the exit door. But the moment they get there, the boys hear it lock. Alex tries his keys to the building to unlock this exit door but none of his keys work. Alex then starts screaming, banging on the door for help.

Then the shadow charges at them. As the boys stand there for a second or two in shock, they decide to run for their lives. They all take off, running and screaming constantly. Amelio then slips on the floor. Running and breathing heavily, Alex and D'Angelo look back and see their friend on the floor in the middle of the hallway. Trying to get up, and reaching his arms out for help, he continues to scream. But his friends' eyes are locked on the dark shadowy figure that grabs Amelio's legs. Amelio, in an attempt to keep himself steady, anchors his fingers into the wooden hallway floor, pulling for help. But his fingernails pop away from his fingers, and blood comes oozing out from his fingers with tiny wood splints flying into his face, into his screaming mouth. The pulling force of the ghost overpowers Amelio's efforts. To escape from the invisible hands of this freaking monster that has managed to terrorize Alex and his friends, Amelio fights back like a bull. He's 6'3", 230 pounds, a star offensive lineman of his high school football team, and definitely not a punk. D'Angelo and Alex run back toward Amelio, trying to help save him they manage to get one of his arms. But then this thing started pulling their friend in the freaking air, lifting him up. It feels like they are playing tug of war, screaming.

"Let him go!" shouts Alex, "Come on, fight, Amelio!" Alex and D'Angelo fell to the ground and when they look around, Amelio is gone, nowhere to be seen. Scared out of their minds and panting heavily, the boys look in the direction of where they had been fighting to save Amelio. That's when white fog slowly comes toward them. Having experienced this scenario before, the two boys head for the light near the door. They slam their bodies repeatedly against it and when it finally opens up, they hop into D'Angelo's car. They peddle to the metal into the dark cold wet early morning. They're screaming, slapping high-fives, but then suddenly remember that they've left their friend Amelio behind. Not sure whether he is still alive or not, the two begin to freak out.

"What do we do, dude? How do we go back in?" yells Alex.

"I don't know man, I don't know!" D'Angelo yells back, equally tensed.

Their last memory of their friend was him desperately pleading them to save him. His tears, his screams, his bloodied fingers, and the tiny wood chips flying all over his face into his crying eyes and mouth were etched in their memories.

While still contemplating what to do, Alex looks in the rear-view mirror and sees Amelio in the second-floor window. Banging on the window and screaming for help, suddenly his body is pulled out of sight, away from the window. As he disappears, the lights of the room that he was in go off as well. That's when Alex and D'Angelo drive out of sight of the school. Alex lifts his hands and silently prays for Amelio, murmuring, "We will be back for you, my friend."

* * *

After driving for about 20 minutes, Alex and D'Angelo try to figure out how to report the incident to the police. "If we tell the police what really happened, if we told the truth about the janitor ghost, they would probably admit us to a psychic ward in town," said Alex.

"Alex, dude, how about we tell half the truth?" replied D'Angelo.

"What do you mean?"

"I mean, we can just say that we got chased around in the school and that Amelio got kidnapped while we were being chased."

"That seems reasonable. Let's do it. Let's inform the police right now," replied Alex confidently.

After informing the police, the two boys head toward the school. When they arrive at the school with the cops, they're hoping to find all the strange things that they experienced earlier. But when the police got inside the school, they do not find anything out of the ordinary. In fact, everything seems perfectly in place, not a spot or stain anywhere.

"Everything seems in order here, boys," says one of the cops. "If you don't hear from your friend Amelio or if he doesn't show up for the next two days, then we will start taking action," he continues, "Come by the police station with Amelio's parents and file a report for a missing person in forty-eight hours."

Sadly, the two boys are unable to even provide a description of the suspected person chasing them because they were too afraid of describing a 6'3" dark ghost, a crazy killer.

When the cops leave, the two boys get into their car and drive off too. During his ride back home, Alex says to himself, "This is so damn frustrating. Something has got to be done."

* * *

A few hours pass by since Amelio's disappearance. But no one knows what really happened to him except for his two friends. They both feel awful for keeping this integral information about what really happened to them. But they continue to keep their mouths sealed. They keep the truth to themselves, knowing everyone would look at them like they had some mental problems, or they might just say they were making up a false story.

Even though we couldn't really get much help trying to find our friend, thinks Alex, *"that is not going to stop me from figuring out how to get Amelio out of the Palmyra High School."* Seeing D'Angelo sitting on the floor in Alex's home, playing video games, Alex thinks, *There has got to be some way. I need to do something so that we still make it to the camp for our spring break party on time.*

Thinking these thoughts, Alex pulls out his cell phone. He starts looking over his saved research on the Palmyra High School. As he scrolls, old newspaper articles start appearing on the screen. He clicks on one of them and finds out that an old janitor died in the building a few years back. The cause of death stated in the newspaper was "heart attack." After finding this out, Alex's mind starts racing as to what to do.

The next thing Alex Googles is the ways of getting rid of bad spirits and ghosts.

But as for D'Angelo, he has had enough. He pauses the game, looks at Alex, who is sitting on his bed with a confused look on his face, and then says, "Dude, would you stop worrying? I think we should head to the camp party and let the police go to the school and find Amelio."

"No, I must do something, brother. I cannot just pretend like nothing happened. I cannot forget his screams... his bloodied fingers... it's just too much," replies Alex, concerned.

"And neither can I, Alex," replies D'Angelo and then continues, "But remember what the police said, we need to wait for the next forty-eight hours. Till then, hold your horses, and try to chill, okay man?"

"I can't. I'm sorry, but I just can't let it go. I need to get to the bottom of the matter, dude, before it's too late," replies Alex after a while.

"You know what, you're really being stupid, trying to do the police's job!" With that, D'Angelo grabs his keys and heads home.

Alex doesn't try to stop him. Instead, he decides to pull out his cell phone and text a few of his friends, telling them what really happened. He tells them everything—the ghost, the weird thick fog, the sticky vomit-like substance, all of it, and more. He ends the text telling them Amelio might be alive. That's because every time he dials Amelio's number, constant heavy breathing is heard at the other end. When Alex dials his number back, an image of the ghostly figure appears on his phone. "I know he's trying to communicate with me," Alex messages his friends, "He needs our help getting him away from this monster that is keeping him at the school."

Surprisingly, the messages that Alex receives on his cell are positive. His friends show their immense support, agreeing to find

Amelio. The first schoolmate to respond is a girl named Martha. Martha was Amelio's first-ever girlfriend, back in the ninth grade. They even had sex during a football game once in a portable toilet.

Martha gets pretty upset when Alex tells her that Amelio was kidnapped, hopefully not dead. She instantly begins crying, and Alex tries his best to calm her down.

Soon Martha shows up at Alex's house and is ready to help him out. She also brings Alex's buddy, James, who comes along with his nosey girlfriend Crystal. Then there is Alex's old girlfriend, Marie, who he can always depend on in case of any emergency.

Alex feels the more people, the better chance they have of finding Amelio. So, he rings up Brandon, an old buddy of his. He's got over 20 football scholarship offers, from Alabama and Nebraska to USC. The dude is huge, 6'5", and plays left tackle for Alex's high school varsity team. Brandon is strong as an ox when they were 10 years old. He would rascal young 100-pound calves to the ground. He's a cool guy, will give his friend the shirt off his back. They often went fishing during the summer months together.

Alex explains to him the whole situation and already knows his friend will be willing to go without caring much about the details.

He doesn't even let Alex finish explaining and said, "Say no more, Alex. I'm on my way to your place."

So, everybody's at Alex's house at about 11 a.m. Alex reminds everyone what they are getting themselves into. They double up in their pickup trucks, drive over to their local hardware store, and load their backpacks with flashlights, batteries, purchased hatchets, mace, and ropes for everyone. James had two baseball bats in the back of his pickup.

Before heading off to the school, Alex gives D'Angelo a call. His cell rings a couple of times, but no one answers. Alex calls one more time, and he picks up, "What's up, Alex? Hope you are not calling me about Amelio. I told you that situation is all bad and just let his parents and cops handle that freaking nightmare," says D'Angelo.

That's when Alex tells him about his plan. He tells him he is going back to the Palmyra High School, along with five other people, to find Amelio. "I have done my research on the building dude, and how to get rid of spirits and the ghost," Alex tells D'Angelo, trying to make him agree to join the group too. He then says, "I am all prepared this time. I have everything that I need. Which is why I would really like you to tag along."

"Dude, you are crazy, but I am not. I am not going back to that hell house. Peace out!" With that, D'Angelo hangs up the phone.

Alex had a strange feeling D'Angelo was going to do that, so he had to come up with another plan to drag D'Angelo down to the school. *I know I need him because he's the only person who knows what to expect other than myself. He won't be as shocked,* thinks Alex to himself. *He can calm the others and navigate the situation.*

With these thoughts running through his mind, Alex slowly walks back to the group where they are having the meeting. "Now, I want to talk about how we're going to get D'Angelo to come down to Palmyra," says Alex. Then he explains to them that D'Angelo knows the place just as well as Alex does. He also tells them how D'Angelo will make their group stronger, if only they can find a way to get him to come down to the school.

Alex asks everyone if they have any ideas. Everyone looks at him with a blank expression, confusion evident on their faces. One could hear crickets in the background but no one had any ideas. Then Alex just throws his idea on the table and says, "Boys and girls, who's down to go to D'Angelo's house and kidnap him?"

Everyone looks at Alex sideways and unanimously declare him crazy. Alex smiles and kind of laughs and agrees, saying, "I know, I know it's a little crazy but the way things are looking, we don't have much of a choice." Then he says, "I am asking you guys again if anybody has a better plan of persuading D'Angelo to come with us to the school." But there were still no answers.

Then Alex continues, "I suggest we all just drive over near his house, how about that?" Everyone shrugs their shoulders and look at each other. Then they all agree.

It's almost noon, and they need to really get over to the school. When there is still no call back from D'Angelo, Alex thinks he's blocking his number. D'Angelo lives with his mom and dad (who just happens to be out of the town for the weekend), in a nice little two-story house that has three bedrooms and a garage that connected to the house. So, Alex tells James and Crystal to go look around the house and see if there are any open windows or other ways of entering without breaking the windows or using a crowbar. "No forced entry," he says with finality in his voice.

After about 10 minutes, James and Crystal run back, telling Alex they saw D'Angelo playing video games in the back-dining room.

"Did he have his headphones on?" asks Alex.

James replies in the affirmative, saying, "He's pretty much in a zone, bobbing his head side to side, laughing at the television screen. So, whatever we do, we all have a better chance of him not hearing us."

The other thing James and Crystal say is that they saw a window barely open by the garage and that there might be a chance of getting through that entrance. "Other than that, everything was locked up tight," says Crystal.

"All right guys, that'll do," says Alex confidently.

CHAPTER 5

Deadly Revenge

ALEX GETS THRILLED ABOUT THE INFORMATION PRO-
vided to him by James and Crystal. After contemplating over the
situation for a few seconds, Alex directs his attention towards the
group and says, "All right, guys! Let's go do this while we still have
the chance."

The six boys and girls get off the car and start walking towards
D'Angelo's house. But then, out of the blue, Martha stops walking.
She hesitates and then says, "I don't understand why but I don't feel
like doing this, guys." After a brief pause, she continues, "How about
you guys meet me at the school, for all we know, Amelio might just
be outside the school or walking home."

Listening to her opinion, Marie too gets the courage to express her feelings. She says, "Honestly, even I don't want to be a part of breaking into D'Angelo's house. Wouldn't it be better if the two of us just stay in the car and wait for you guys to return?"

Martha and Marie's reluctance to go inside D'Angelo's house forces Alex to say, "All right, if that's what you both want." He continues, "Wait for us in the car, have your phones charged up because I'll text you to pull the car up in the garage when the ride is needed."

Martha and Marie go back to the car while Alex, Brandon, James, and Crystal sneak up to the cracked window. Alex takes a close look at it and is relieved to see that it's not locked. He pushes the rusted frame and tries to open the window, but it accidentally shuts. Without further delay, Alex and James try to open it but once again, it snaps shuts, making a huge crashing sound. Good for them, D'Angelo can't hear a thing at this point. They hear laughter and screams as D'Angelo keeps playing, pounding the floor with his fist. He's too busy playing his military game with several other online players and has both ears plugged up. When the window finally opens, they all sneak through the window as quietly as possible.

After getting into the garage, Alex tells James to look for some rope and duct tape while he himself looks for something that'll help him knock out D'Angelo. "I hope I find a bat or shovel," mutters Alex to himself. James finds some rope, and Alex succeeds in finding a kids' plastic baseball bat, hard enough to make D'Angelo unconscious temporarily. He swings it against a wooden workbench in the garage and notices that it doesn't make a dent. Alex whispers to his friends, "Hey, this will do the job without accidentally killing my friend." Brandon finds some duct tape. Alex then tells Brandon to watch out the window just in case somebody pulls up while he, along with James and Crystal, sneaks his way into D'Angelo's house.

As they sneak in the door that's connected to the house, they find themselves in the kitchen. They stop and look straight ahead where they see D'Angelo playing, totally engaged in his game, completely distracted. They all tiptoe to D'Angelo as he's deep into the game. Slowly, Alex walks up behind him with the bat. He takes a half swing at the back of his head, "Bow!" The sound is so loud Alex's ears experiences a slight ring. As D'Angelo's head and body flop on the den carpet, Alex starts having second thoughts for doing all this to his friend. The left side of D'Angelo's headphones shatters all over the room. His eyes buck as if they are about to pop out of his face. "Oh shit! Alex! You killed him! You killed him!" panics Crystal, "Martha and Marie were right. This is a bad, bad idea!"

Hearing the shrills, Brandon too comes inside. He puts his hand over Crystal's mouth. She starts to kick, screaming in his hand with tears coming down her cheeks. Then she bites Brandon's hand so hard that a thin streak of fresh blood slides between his hand and her chin. The words that were earlier muffled by Brandon's hand are heard clearly the moment Brandon slumps on the floor. As Alex checks D'Angelo's pulse, he looks up at everybody and whispers, "He is going to be all right, just relax."

Alex realizes how deeply involved they have gotten themselves into this conundrum. They all stare at each other in shock, completely silent, unaware of what to do next. All one could hear was the voices of the people on D'Angelo's headset. These people, who had been playing the game with D'Angelo, kept calling his name repeatedly. Alex hurriedly unplugs his interactive gaming box. Telling James to move fast, he quickly ties D'Angelo up. He puts the duct tape on his mouth before he wakes up from his daze.

Crystal starts crying. She puts her hands over her face, then says to Alex, "Why did you have to hit him so hard!" Alex continues to tie D'Angelo. He then says, "Crystal, I only took a half-swing. And it was only a kid's toy! It was a plastic bat!" Then he texts Martha and Marie to back her SUV into the garage, which Alex was about to open. They haul D'Angelo into the back of the SUV. They close the door and wait inside the closed garage.

James quickly cleans up the broken headset. In fact, he puts what's left in his backpack. He makes sure everything is in its original place inside D'Angelo's parents' home, so he closes and locks the garage door window.

Everyone gets their composure, waiting for Brandon to meet them in the SUV. Once he joins them, they pull out. They close the garage by using a reserve clicker they had found in the den.

Closing the garage door, the group divides into two cars, and then drives off to Palmyra High School. Alex's ex-girlfriend Marie sits with Brandon in his Ford F150 truck. In Martha's SUV, Alex sits in the back seat with D'Angelo while James, Crystal, and Martha fill up the car's front seats. Then the two cars stop on the road in a wooded area toward the school and switch D'Angelo from the SUV to the F150 truck.

Now that they are halfway to the school, Alex decides to try waking D'Angelo. Alex shakes him, slaps him a few times while constantly yelling his name in his ear, but all in vain. Although D'Angelo is breathing and moans from time to time, he doesn't respond.

Getting closer to Palmyra High School, they discuss what to do with D'Angelo. Alex says, "Feels as if we are going to do away with his body for good." But then, listening to everyone's suggestion of dropping his body off, Alex says to the group, "Chill out, guys! He's not dead. Let's just leave him in the car till we leave the school." Seeing his friends' nervousness, he continues, "Look, we're probably only going to be in the school no more than thirty minutes. All we have to do is find Amelio, get my car keys and get back to D'Angelo." Everyone agrees, appreciating Alex's excellent idea.

The closer they got to Palmyra, the more nervous Alex gets. He doesn't know what's going to happen. At this point, he looks at his watch and notices that it's 5 p.m. Alex just hopes he doesn't end up like Amelio, or any of them, for that matter. Going through the whole incident that took place earlier makes his heart ache.

They pull to the school, and Alex sees that his SUV is still parked in the parking lot. D'Angelo is still knocked out, more like snoring loud in a deep sleep. Marie takes out a paper, writes a nice little note, saying, *"We all love you, D'Angelo. Call us from your cell phone the moment you wake up. We may need your help."*

Once Marie is done writing the note, they all hop out of their vehicles. Staring at the building, Alex thinks, *It looks the same as last time.*

They get out, load up their backpacks with hardware store purchases for their protection. Then Alex tells everyone, "Leave all the car windows down and leave your car keys under the car mats of the passenger seat. I don't want us to go through what I did last time and lose our keys." Alex decides not to go through the front door this time. *The obvious entry might cause this ghost freak show to start sooner than we need right now,* thinks Alex to himself.

Alex still has the keys to multiple entrances to the school. He thinks of quitting the job and returning these keys once they get Amelio out of this horror high school.

The only positive thing about their day is that the weather is great. There is an early chilly spring breeze blowing in the air, sun shining, and a few birds chirping. Not a cloud was to be seen in the sky. With no gloves or winter hats, the boys and girls look prepared to go get their friend, completely ready to slay any ghost that comes their way.

Martha, Brandon, James, Crystal, Marie, and Alex walk around the building, hoping to hear Amelio pounding somewhere, making noises, or screaming for help. They're walking and listening. James and Crystal decide to go together to one side of the building and see if they can find the best door to get into the school. James and Crystal have been in a relationship since the ninth grade. They both are not only seniors but have full-ride scholarships to attend the University of Nebraska in the engineering department. They are super smart, which is why they'd greatly help all of their friends pass algebra, physics, and geometry. They are the best of friends one could ever ask for.

Before James and Crystal start searching, Alex says, "Text us if you hear or find something. I will go and look around the place with Marie." Then pointing towards Brandon and Martha, Alex says, "You two go together and search the place. If you find anything, drop a text." After saying that, the three pairs part ways and move toward different directions.

Alex begins his quest with his ex-girlfriend, Marie. The reason why he wanted Marie, and Marie alone, to accompany him was because he still had feelings for her. She'd always been the love of his life, the center of his attention. He would've never left her or broken up with her had he not gotten his daughter's mother pregnant in a moment of weakness at a house party a couple of years ago. This one mistake made him restless for several days and nights. He felt

Marie deserved a better partner, someone who'd be more faithful, more loyal. And although Marie showed a willingness to forgive him and put the whole incident behind them, Alex just felt too guilty, insisting on ending their physical relationship abruptly.

Now, Marie and Alex are the best of friends. He trusts her blindly, and so does she, and at the end of the day, they're good together. As for Martha and Brandon, well, let's just say they were anything but a couple. They are the complete opposite of one another. Brandon has his 20-plus football scholarships. Some even believe he's going to be an NFL draft pick one day. Then there is Martha. She's big into nature and Marie's best friend. She has plans to be a horticulturalist when she graduates from college. She has already been accepted into Texas A&M.

Anyhow, everybody continues to walk around the building. Unfortunately, the group fails to find a door entrance that they believe won't alarm the freak ghost inside. That's when Alex thinks of just using one of his keys at the back-basement entrance. But he soon discards the idea and begins looking for other options.

On the other side of the school, James and Crystal find a window that looks old enough to kick in the hatches. James finds a window crack open that's not locked. The window opening is large enough for them to squeeze through. Crystal tries calling and texting Alex about the window's entry that they've found but notices that there are no network signals. She keeps calling and texting him, but none of her messages reaches Alex.

After trying a couple of times more, Crystal and James decide to just go inside, hoping to meet their friends safely in the building.

Brandon, Martha, Marie, and Alex are having no luck finding a non-door opening into the school building. Brandon complains, "Guys, what do we do now?"

As Brandon is speaking, a baseball-sized rock flies past his face, smashing the window in front of them. They all turn around and see it's Martha, the rock thrower. She says, "Yeah, desperate times call for desperate measures. You guys are taking too long, it's almost evening. We've got to move it along, Alex," says Martha.

After being startled out of their minds, they finally calm down. Then all of them carefully crawl through the broken glass and window. While these four are in the middle of the school hallway, James and Crystal end up in the counselor's room, located on the other side of the building.

"I know the way. Follow me and remember, don't leave the group, or you will be lost," says Alex confidently. They make their way to the double door area that's on the second floor. Walking along the creepy dark hallway, they feel something really weird in there. Soon the place starts getting cold. They grab each other's hands, all four of them feeling that peculiar, uncomfortable sensation of fear.

Looking side by side, turning their heads, watching, a vomit-like pink gooey substance slides down the hallway lockers. The stench smells like vomit and is everywhere. Seeing what was in front of him, Alex says to others, "What even is that? I mean, this is just so ridiculous I'm almost not even scared anymore." After a brief pause, he continues while struggling, "But that stench, it's horrible! Don't know about you guys, but it's definitely getting my breath away. So, so foul!"

Unlike Alex, Martha is crying hysterically, almost pulling Brandon's arm out of his socket. Marie walks over to her. Slapping her in the face, she says, "Will you please stop crying? You need to get it together, Martha, so we can focus on getting Amelio out of this place." Then she looks at the boys and orders, "Everyone, get your axes from your backpacks and be on guard. Let's be prepared for the unexpected."

James and Crystal, the two lovebirds, stick their tounges deep down one another's throats for a long passionate kiss. They hug tightly before continuing walking softly, sneaking and peering in and out of school offices. They continue to hope that they find their friends inside safely. "I wonder where they are," whispers Crystal.

"So, do I," replies James. Holding hands, James and Crystal step into the hallway. Soon they let go of each other's hands as cold air fills the hall, and they end up grabbing their individual bodies. Walking slowly, they turn their heads, looking at the pink, vomit-like substance dripping down the walls.

It's pitch-black dark in the building, only cell and flashlights are available. Brandon, Martha, Marie, and Alex reach for their flashlights, walking around, pointing the light in walkways with an axe in the other hand. From a distance, they see a dark ghostly shadow figure, which makes them all scream. Clinching each other, they freeze for a moment. They're trying to identify the shadowy figure but could not verify.

The shadow moves. Not wanting to be identified, it steps out of the light.

James and Crystal squint. They, too, try to see who and what's lurking in their presence. James and Crystal grab each other's hands as they feel a presence near them. Their bodies shiver from the cold breeze, racing past their bodies into a classroom. The couple softly whispers for Amelio and Alex. A dark ghost-like male figure makes noise in the classroom as it runs through the wall where a classroom whiteboard is hanging, disappearing.

James and Crystal still call Alex's name, thinking he may have been in and out of the classroom. They can't figure out why Alex is not responding to their voice. They text Alex on his cell phone but nothing, no response. They decide to continue their search through the classroom.

Brandon, Martha, Marie, and Alex cross the double doors in the long hallway, waiting for Crystal and James to pop up nearby. They whisper their names, walking very slowly down the long school hallway. Marie starts texting. Her cell phone remains in her hand, hoping to get a response.

James and Crystal continue to follow in the direction of the shadowy figure into the now silent room. Walking quietly on their tiptoes, they keep whispering for Alex, all the while shining their flashlights all over the classroom. While they are looking around in the classroom, a loud thud shudders the room—Bam, Bam. The classroom doors shut so hard everyone in the building hears the sound echo throughout the school. A click follows it, the sound of the classroom doors locking.

James and Crystal's eyes widen, looking at each other. James pulls Crystal close to him and kisses her. When she kisses back, he whispers, "I love you and promise nothing is going to happen to us, Crystal."

"I love you too, James. We're going to get through this together," says Crystal. They look at each other and holding hands, they rush toward the door, trying to open it and then kicking.

They stand at the door, facing each other, too afraid to scream. They both try texting their friends, but their phones catch no signal. Standing at the door while trying to text, James stops halfway. He touches Crystal's hand, motioning her to stop texting. Then he puts his index finger on his lips, and they try to listen to the peculiar noises coming to the classroom.

They hear the sound of heavy footsteps and keys rattling, which get louder and closer with each passing second. Crystal whispers, "Let us quickly find a place to hide somewhere in the classroom only." Crystal crawls forward and squeezes her small frame inside a built-in horizontal bottom cabinet. James hides behind the teacher's desk.

A ghostly shadow appears outside the room, covering the door of the classroom where the couple hides. They hear loud footsteps and the sound of keys jingling. The rusty door of the classroom slowly opens. Crystal bites her nails out of nervousness. Pouring sweat makes her hair stick to her face, makeup drips to her shirt, and her small, chubby face gets warm. Sweating heavily with tears dropping on her fingers, she texts James, "Do you hear that? I had to drop my backpack with my axe to get inside this small space, do you have yours, baby?"

To her message, James responds immediately, saying, "No, my backpack wouldn't fit under this desk. I had to leave it just outside the desk." After a brief pause, he texts again, saying, "I'm trying to reach for it with my leg without making too much noise. Don't text me back, just try to stay quiet. Love you. I'm going to get you out."

James peeps under the desk. His body shivers as he sees two huge wet boot prints on the floor. He watches the person walk around, moving desks and checking behind random objects.

While this is all happening, Alex is texting on his friends' group but is clueless as to where James and Crystal are. "This is so frustrating," he murmurs.

Alex still tries to text Amelio and listen for Crystal and James with his phone. Suddenly, James and Crystal's texts start pouring in. Hopeful, Alex tries to respond but fails. The weird thing is that although Alex can see their texts, every time he tries to text them back, his messages read: "Can't send, no signal." Crystal describes she can't see but can hear the heavy footsteps and objects being pushed around.

Alex closes his eyes, whispering a silent prayer that this sick monster-like ghost will just go away, leaving them to find Amelio and go to their spring break weekend in peace.

Five long minutes slowly tick by as the tall ghostly janitor looks around. Finally giving up, his shadow moves, walking out of the classroom. That's when Alex sees this ghostly spirit for the first time. To his amazement, the mysterious figure looks like an actual human, except for the fact that the outer portions of its body seem to be shaking. There is also a white-purple haze around its body, a square frame, and black military glasses on his face. His left side is totally out of whack.

Alex points to the others. When everyone sees the spirit, they put their hands over their mouths, trembling fearfully. Toward the figure's left side, it seems like the skin is stretched near his ear, the eye is barely open with eyebrow pushing up so high that wrinkles form toward the top of his head. The left lip is pulling toward his chin. On the right side, his bloodshot eye is bucked like it's going to pop out any second. The rest of the right side is drooping. His lips are tightly sealed together, and white drool seeps out the side of his mouth while he stands about 6'3" tall.

Alex and his group see all this in a flash, for merely a few seconds, and while they're still struggling to grasp the severity of the situation, the figure disappears. They watch his body dissolve back into a dark non-descriptive ghostly image, walking out of the classroom where Crystal and James are trembling for their lives.

As the ghost walks out, they manage to crawl inside the school's administrative section, which happens to be all glass, giving them a bird's eye view. At this point, Alex notices that his phone has a signal. Panicked and totally out of his wits, he tries to communicate once again. But this time, instead of texting, he accidentally touches the phone icon, causing Crystal's phone to ring. Alex is ecstatic to hear the call being connected. Everyone crouches down next to him, whispering to his phone, "Crystal, please, answer the phone. Hurry!"

Unfortunately, Crystal's phone is not on silent. It blares a rap ringtone loudly. James starts panicking and covers his mouth with his hand. Crystal tries her best to put her phone on silent, but it's too late. The dark ghostly male image walks back into the room, looks at the lower closet, gets on two knees, and starts sniffing the room. He looks over at Crystal's backpack, pulls it toward him, and after unzipping, he pulls out her axe.

A partial image of his face flashes in and out of focus for James, who is watching from under the desk, completely terrified. The ghostly apparition slowly gets low, crawls on his knees while dragging Crystal's axe in one hand. He then pulls his body with his elbows and creeps toward the lower cabinet at a snail's pace.

Crystal's cell phone that is now on vibrate, keeps buzzing repeatedly with Alex and James's texts. Cell phone in one hand and her second hand covering her mouth, tears stream from her face continuously. Unaware of what is happening outside or all that was going to happen, Crystal remains in the dark.

Now lying on his stomach, the ghostly figure stares at the lower cabinet where Crystal is shaking, her lips moving and hands formed in prayer as she prays for a miracle. The ghost crawls closer to the cabinet and then knocks on her door twice. James screams in the palm of his hands while covering his mouth, crying nonstop. A cool chilling mist floats throughout the room as the ghost slowly starts rising up from the floor. With the axe's handle in both hands, he bends slightly down. Then, aiming the axe's sharp edge at the cabinet, he winds it up to his back, and slamming through the cabinet, strikes Crystal's mid-section. The axe breaks the wood, and blood gushes out. Crystal's still alive but keeps screaming frantically as blood oozes from her eyes and mouth.

After throwing up in his hand and pissing and defecating all over himself, James remains under the desk, shaking in horror. Tears stream down his face, snot everywhere, completely unaware of what to do. It's as if the unnerving terror has frozen him. He is in a cold body shock, sweating uncontrollably and his heart racing beyond control. Then quickly, James darts from beneath the desk and grabs his axe and mace. He runs over, trying to strike the ghostly figure in his back. But much to his surprise, his axe goes through the ghost's body, sticking in the floor after penetrating the carpet and hardwood floor.

While striking Crystal's body, the image turns his head around. When he looks James directly into his eyes, he points his middle finger at James, signaling for him to move back. James runs out of the classroom into the hallway. As the ghost takes a final swing with his axe, he hits it into Crystal's throat, causing her tongue and eyes to pop out of her face onto the floor. Blood covers the classroom floor. Soaking the carpet, it slowly pours into the school hallway.

Crystal's cell phone continues buzzing with the message: "Hang in there, we're going to help you."

CHAPTER 6

From the Diary

LOUD BARKING ALONG WITH RAPID SCRATCHING OUT-
side my front door alerts me at once. When I look outside, through
the window, I see it's Chester. I open the door and am surprised to
see the black composition book lying at my entrance door. I look at
Chester, thinking perhaps I had accidentally dropped this book after
being distracted or something. Ignoring these thoughts, I wipe off
the mysterious black book, grab my pipe and start reading, all the
time thinking to myself, *This is unbelievable.*

Oddly, the ink on the pages starts changing colors. The writing appears from black to what looks like red ink, but strangely, it's
a darker thick red ink with splatters on the following pages. As I

continue to read the description from Biff, the tormented ghost janitor's composition book, it takes my breath away. I am just not accustomed to reading books like this one. But now that I've started reading it, it's almost impossible for me to put it away.

In the book, inside a moonlit empty classroom, sits the dark ghostly image of Biff at a student-size classroom desk. He writes with his bloody index finger, recording his first deadly revengeful encounter intently. The ghost expresses his inner emotions, writing about the joy and exhilaration felt by his most recent killing. Blood-red tears of joy dripping from his eyes' tear ducts, he smiles, recording his story as small splatters drip onto the white portions of his pages every now and then. He describes the feeling of euphoria, his adrenaline rush of presuming death, how the killing was better than having sex with his once wife.

Biff lingers on in his composition. He writes about his love for the smell of fear and that of underarm sweat, the secretion glands of his helpless victims. In pursuit of his human prey, he says his tongue tastes their fear in the air. Their sweat gives him an adrenaline rush, and the taste of fear reminds him of spoiled meat.

As I continue reading, I observe how this guy is obsessed with creating fear because, after his accidental death, he lost the choice to control his personal anxiety from taking hold of him as a human being does naturally.

Moments later, his ghostly dark figure gets up. With the book in his hand, he walks through a classroom whiteboard, black smoke morphing through the side of the high school building. His black spirit drifts outside into the late evening sunset air.

Midnight displays on a kitchen clock as his dark figure walks through the locked front door of his old half-burnt house. The ghostly male shadow walks into its once bedroom, placing his composition book on his old bedroom desk. His dark spirit shadow lingers in the room, walking around, looking at the room where he once lived, as a mortal, a normal human. He sits on his former king-size bed with his hands on his knees. The room becomes cold and white misty condensation breath is seen from his nostrils. Minutes later, an SUV ride-sharing vehicle pulls up to the house. When it stops in front of the house, Ariel exits the vehicle and enters her partially-damaged home. After lighting several candles, she walks into her master bedroom and immediately recognizes the black composition book.

Feeling the coldness of the room, Ariel rubs her hands together. Blowing warm air from her mouth, she picks up her husband's composition book from the desk. She pulls it to her chest using a firm grip as tears stream down her closed eyes. She looks at it, smells it. Then she drops the book on the dusty floor, and as she does that, red beetles scatter from underneath the composition book. Picking it up again, she skims through the pages and notices a new section written in red. Ariel reads her husband's psychopathic lust for revenge and the reason behind his death. Whispering, "No, no, honey no," she walks into her dining room designing alter. Next, she takes a dozen candles from her kitchen cabinets and places them in a large circle on the table, lighting them all. After that, she places a large white cross in the center. Then she picks up a tightly wrapped bundle of sage, burns it to a steady flow of continuous sage smoke, flowing throughout the room. She walks over to her kitchen's spice rack and takes out the sea saltbox. She walks through her living room area and starts pouring salt along the walls of her room.

Soon, a white barrier, a perimeter is formed. Thereafter, she begins spraying saltwater throughout the room.

Inside the bedroom, Biff's ghostly figure stands up and starts moving the furniture. He begins stamping the bedroom floor, and then crouching his large dark frame begins crawling the walls and bedroom ceiling.

Ariel grabs the Bible in one hand and her husband's composition book in the other. She falls on both knees, holding both books in the air. "Honey, I know you hear me, baby, I'm so sorry your death was tragically ended, so sudden, catching you by surprise. I know you wanted to be home for our special dinner that night, we have thousands of great memories that will last an eternity. Soon we will be together again. But that's not going to happen if you don't let go of this demon that wants to keep us apart. All you have to do is remember 1 John 1:9." She drops the composition book and opens her Bible. "If we confess our sins, he is faithful and just to forgive us our sins, and cleanse us from all unrighteousness," continues Ariel. She falls on her face sobbing, screaming for Biff to please repent, pleading with God to give him a chance to save his soul from damnation.

There is neither a response nor any sign of paranormal activity in her living room. However, in the bedroom, the dark, human-like ghostly figure stops running up and down the ceiling and walls. He drops his body to the floor, then ascends his dark ghostly body to the ceiling, morphing through it and leaving a cloud of thick black smoke. The house inside is completely quiet, with no sound against the backdrop of a full moon. Ariel sits at the dining room table and takes off her glasses. With her head down, crying softly, and pounding the table, she gathers herself.

Moments later, Ariel calls a ride-share service. Before it arrives, she blows out the candles, takes her dead husband's composition book back to the bedroom, and places it on the desk. Then she steps out the front door and, locking it, walks past the for-sale sign back into her ride-share transportation.

Nighttime ticks into the early A.M. hours. A full moon reflects a steady drizzle. A soft wind blows trees, swirling wind howling from a distance. The ghost describes a slim, four-legged animals' eyes are seen running toward the house. The animal leaps through the open bedroom window, grabs the book, leaps out through the bedroom window, racing back. This time of the year, with a few weeks from spring, the weather in Nebraska is just perfect—averaging between 40–60 degrees, cool nights, and a little rain, some light snow occasionally.

I scan the pages of what appears to be an epic story of revenge, human survival, and the struggle to keep a demon spirit from destroying the soul of a former Navy sailor and beloved high school custodian. The writing also shows an unbelievable terror between young, mentally underdeveloped, and psychologically challenged high school students. The instigating kids come across as scared and starving for attention. I read sections describing these delinquent kids displaying their lack of self-esteem as high school adolescents.

Their behavior seems to have pissed off a once stable janitor; what a sad mess.

Once again, I just find it extremely difficult to understand this bizarre, horrifying fiction and the correlation this book has with my Doberman. Exhausted and a bit depressed, I decide to turn in this time. I immediately put the book in my top office desk drawer. After locking it with my key, I take a shower and fall into a deep slumber.

* * *

During the early hours of the morning, I wake up to Chester shaking, whining, making subtle noises. I soon realize he appears to be having a nightmare. I fall asleep again and wake up late in the morning. I observe the keys are off my desk with dirty dog paw prints on the desk chair and the drawer where I placed the composition book.

That's when I recall reading last night about a four-legged animal sprinting towards Palmyra High School, where it meets the ghost in the middle of the high school's football field. Taking the composition book out of the four-legged animal's mouth, the animal takes off back to its dwelling, running with the speed of a racehorse.

I'm looking at my notes taken from the janitor's composition book while trying to trace his patterns as I recant. The dark ghostly

janitor figure walks through the school building walls and continues reigning terror on the kids now trapped in the school by his
ghostly powers.

As I read this story more, supernatural occurrences start happening inside my home once again. Plumbing in my house rattles,
and I hear plastic pipes along with the copper tubes shaking. All the
sink faucets start spewing black water. Plates in the kitchen fly out of
the cabinets. Steak knives zooming toward my location whistle past
my head as I duck down in fear. Again, I find myself crawling on the
floor praying for deliverance. All the noise in the house makes my
heart tremble. The kitchen cabinets and the doors throughout the
house keep opening and closing. The toilets in bathrooms continue
flapping up and down. This time I crawl, not in fear of this supernatural force but to protect myself from getting hit by flying objects. I
crawl to my garage door and struggle to push it open. Once I suc-
ceed, I get into my expensive, powerful 4x4 pickup truck. The accel-
erator bursting, I drive through my wooden garage door, screaming
down the road. I pull over to a nearby pond on my estate, get out of
the car, and just sit out on the grass to calm my nerves. Staring at the
pond, I start throwing rocks, making ripples.

* * *

Moments later, my eyes open up. Slowly pushing my body off the grass, I notice a silhouette of a tall man holding a mop, accompanied by a dog with long ears and a big nose. It looks like a Doberman, but before I could take a look at it properly and figure out the complete image, the silhouette disappears. My first reaction is to turn in a 360-degree angle, but nothing. Then within seconds, the temperature gets so cold it starts hailing—grapefruit-size hail. Hail this size...in the middle of spring! I scream out loud, "Hey! Who is there? Chester? Are you there?" But I can't hear myself talking. It's as though I'm deaf. I scream, jump up and down, throwing rocks in the pond, but the image is still in the pond. This goes on for at least five minutes but then suddenly, I hear my screams, and the image disappears; two bats fly away into the wooded area nearby. Totally freaked out, I hop into my damaged truck, but it won't start. I get out, open the hood of the vehicle, and as soon as I drop the hood, my truck starts without me, or anyone, being inside.

As I'm getting into the truck, I feel the weight of an object landing on the truck's flatbed. When I look back, it's Chester. "Damn, I'm having such a serious moment, if this dog of mine could talk, we would be having words," I say to myself. He is displaying an extreme level of excitement, leaping from the flatbed to the ground, four feet up and down, back to the flatbed, he is amazing. After all the dog gymnastics, I get licked in the face. Once in the truck, I head back home to deal with the bizarre occurrences. I feel my home is taken over by what I assume is some supernatural demon force.

Surprisingly, when I arrive back, it's as though nothing ever happened. *Am I losing it? Was I hallucinating, or is this book hypnotizing me, taking me into some supernatural parallel universe? Whatever is happening! I've got to figure this out.*

The level of intense fear I experienced, in addition to having no control of the situation, is crazy. All this is centered around strange disappearances, behavior, and mannerisms from my brilliant Doberman. I'm wondering if there is a connection between my Doberman and the four-legged animal that Biff talks about in his composition book.

CHAPTER 7

Alex's Battle of Terror

EVENING TURNS INTO NIGHT AND NIGHT INTO MID-night, but Alex and his group remain trapped within the Palmyra High School premises. Still searching for Amelio and wandering across the building, it turns 4 a.m. but sadly, not a peep from the missing person.

After witnessing Crystal's tragic death, James totally breaks down. Looking at him, one would think he has completely frozen in his place, with unbelievably pale skin and zero capacity to move or function. Squatting down in the corner of the long hallway, James does not want to move or breathe. At that moment, he aspired to cease to exist. If the love of his life was not by his side anymore, he didn't wish to be alive either.

While James struggles with his inner turmoil, Alex and his team stay crouched in the administration office, listening to the loud noises of bathroom toilets flushing, one right after the other. These flushing sounds keep echoing off the school walls. Toilet tops continue banging up and down, making a *pop, pop* sound so loud the group starts complaining to each other about getting headaches. "I really want to find James and Crystal, I really want to wait, but it's time to move ahead guys," says Alex loudly, trying to be heard over all the noise. "Plus, neither is responding to their text. We've got to go before we get trapped in this room," continues Alex. Brandon chimes in, "I think so too. Let's push forward."

To this, Marie reacts with frustration, "Please, guys, don't say that. We must not give up hope. Let us stay put a little longer." After listening to her, Alex responds, "We are no good for anybody if we don't save ourselves, Marie. Remember, James and Crystal can be anywhere in the building. We have to think about ourselves so that we rescue Amelio." After a small discussion, they all agree that staying in one place is not the greatest of ideas, especially with a psycho ghost janitor prowling around in the school.

Just as they are about to move ahead, a buzzing cell phone gets Alex's attention. To his surprise, it's James, crawling on all fours in the hallway. Alex sees him move at a snail's pace with his backpack strapped to his back, and a large axe in one of his hands. He's going in and out of offices, peeking his head out, listening and watching his surrounding as he tries to find an exit.

Whispering words of motivation to himself and moving from one room to another room, James slides across the long hallway. While rolling into a classroom, his axe slips out of his hand. Flying across the classroom and at a distance, the axe lands between Martha's legs, which startles her. That's when she, along with Brandon, sees James. Although this little episode of the axe landing near her body leaves her astounded, she is relieved to find out that at least James is alive and seemingly well. Thankful for being together, they all move now.

While moving slowly, Alex whispers to his friends, "At least we're all together now." With fear and uncertainty apparent in his voice, he continues, "With one another's support, I'm sure we'll get out of this place."

Then Alex asks James in a quiet voice, "Dude, where is Crystal? You two were together, were you not?" But before James could respond, a loud *clack, clack* sound interrupts them. The same sound keeps coming from various rooms and the school's heating and cooling ventilation systems. They look around, waiting to see Amelio.

James moves slowly away from a classroom vent, tippy-toeing his way to a nearby closet. Sweating bullets, he feels his heart is about to beat out his chest. He makes it to a closet and nervously reaches his hand to its knob. He slowly opens the door, not knowing what to expect. As soon as he opens the door of the closet, blood starts running down its wooden door. As he sees Crystal's axe in the center of her head, large puddles of blood bubble up from the closet floor.

Seeing such a horrible sight forces James to jump back in shock. But as he's stepping back, he slips and falls on the pool of blood as more blood falls from Crystal's mouth.

"Oh God, help him, please, this is so awful," screams Martha as she looks at the pool of blood. "Where is this blood coming from, James?" shouts Martha, who is unable to see what is present before James.

As James struggles to get up from the floor, now all sticky and slippery because of the blood, he busts his head on the tile floor. Trying to get up, he continuously slips, rolling around in Crystal's blood. Trying his best to get out of it, he finally crawls away from it to the nearest classroom desk.

Crying hysterically about seeing Crystal's head stuck to the closet wall earlier, James completely loses his composure. Alex, Marie, Martha, and Brandon try to get to James, but the blood is streaming toward them.

Now, they're in the same messy, gross situation, trying with all their strengths to get the hell out of that room. That's when James starts getting dizzy. He begins hyperventilating, complaining he can't breathe. "I just want to die. It's too much! Just look at her and look at me. Show your face, you coward of a ghost! I'm not afraid of you! I'll kick your ass for what you did to my girl," says a tearful James. A best friend and girlfriend brutally murdered in front of his eyes. James will never be the same if he makes it out of this alive.

It took a while, but he finally gets the courage to get himself together. He wipes the tears from his eyes which are still bloody and manages to close the closet door. Then taking a deep breath hysterically, he wanders off in the hall, following the rest. That's when James realizes that their group of six has lost an important member. The rest of their journey will be without Crystal, the spark and shine of the group. She took with her the light of the heavens, darkening the world behind.

Alex, Martha, Marie, James, Brandon, and perhaps Amelio too, who Alex prays in his heart is still alive, are present somewhere in this building. They continue their mission to find Amelio, hoping to stay alive in the process. They walk down the frightful hallways, one after the other.

While still wandering, their eyes start tearing from a repulsive odor that burns out their eyes, causing them to cough uncontrollably. They walk along the hallway. Martha is about to throw up, so she runs over to a nearby water fountain. Trying to send it back down her throat, she grabs her stomach. Unable to stand the stench, she then runs to a nearby locker, opens it, and hurls pink chunks of something no one has ever seen before.

"Oh shit, it's black squiggly worms!" says Alex. Yes, squiggly because if they weren't moving, they'd just be gummy worms.

Alex continues, "See, these are moving, crawling down the locker through the runny vomit she just blew out of her mouth! What a gross mess! Martha? How are you holding up? The smell is just unbearable."

They all feel like hurling. That's when Brandon complains, "Man! The odor is making the hair inside my nose burn! What's up? Does it always stink worse than a skunk?"

Once Martha stops throwing up everywhere, they all take out their jackets, pullovers, or some type of extra clothing, covering their faces to help themselves with the awful smell. But it really doesn't work. The smell just seeps through the clothing. Martha starts throwing up again inside her makeshift facial covering made from her sweater. Now the vomit is all over her shirt, down to her shoes. They all are coughing and complaining about how bad their heads hurt while simultaneously trying to walk along the hallway, still in pursuit of Amelio.

Spitting out black worms and vomit, Martha eyes a nearby girls' restroom in the school's hallway. On the other hand, James decides he's got to go to the school's boy's bathroom to take a much complained-about number two dump.

Martha takes off, running into the bathroom to finish throwing up and cleaning herself up at the sink. Brandon walks to the door right behind her. After giving it a couple of knocks, he says, "Martha, are you okay?" As the sound of the running water continues, paper towels can be heard rapidly being pulled. Martha wipes away the chunks of vomit and dead worms—a few still wriggling on the floor, down the drain of her sink.

Martha replies, "I'm doing okay. I just stopped puking, feeling much better now. Getting cleaned up at the moment. You guys, please wait for me. I'm so scared, but I do feel so much better." While talking, she takes off her shoes and rinses them in the sink.

Nervous and cautious, Alex and his group wait patiently outside while Martha labors to get rid of her penetrating vomit. She tries to clean the stains on her clothing, under her fingernails, behind her ears, and inside her hair. She constantly blows her nose as if for something other than pink vomit and worms. Martha grabs more paper towels. Then she looks at herself in the mirror, rinsing her face. Putting on eye shadow, makeup, lip gloss, she sprays herself with some perfume.

"Throwing up on myself was so embarrassing, I have to walk out of this bathroom looking good and smelling good," says Martha to herself.

Out from the corner of her eye, she notices a glimpse of a dark shadowy figure. Then stopping for a moment, she quickly turns her body in the direction of the imagined shadowy figure.

Still waiting outside her door, Martha's friends hear her scream at the top of her lungs, "Oh my god, oh my god!" Panicked, her friends run closer to the door, knocking and screaming her name, asking if she was okay. But there was complete silence on the other side.

After a while, Martha finally responds, "I'm okay, just a little edgy. I feel like my mind is playing tricks. I'll be coming out to join the group in a few minutes, guys."

Smoothing clear lip gloss over her previously dawned red lipstick, Martha's eyebrows move up. She stops midway, listening to a faint, whispering noise bouncing off the restroom walls. "Hey there, beautiful girl, mmm, mmm," says a whispering voice.

Martha's eyes race side to side, and she attempts to understand what she thinks was just whispered in her presence. Slowly yet methodically grabbing the makeup items and putting them back in her backpack, she looks around the restroom. Then slowly pulling out her mace and flashlight, she tiptoes to the restroom exit.

"Hey beautiful, where you're going, huh?" repeats the whispering voice.

Ignoring the creepy voices, Martha tries to exit the bathroom but finds it locked. Pounding on the restroom door, Martha belts out, tears rolling down her cheeks, "Guys, push the door open. It's not opening on my side! Help me get out of here!" Alex and his friends start panicking. They scream back to Martha, saying, "We'll get you out, Martha, stay put!"

Alex, Marie, and Brandon push with everything. "We must help her open this simple bathroom door," orders Alex. Across the way, James comes running down the hallway. Tripping and then coming to his two feet, he tries to pull up his pants along with taking out a stream of brown and white toilet paper from of his underwear, "I heard the screams! What's going on? I'm on my way, guys," says James.

Martha stands in the middle of the high school bathroom, crying as makeup and mascara smear and drip on her face. Alex notices the sign on the door reading: Faculty and staff.

This restroom is only equipped for one person at a time, which is why it's quite intimate and very small, thinks Alex.

"Don't worry, Martha. I'm going to help you get out of here," says the whispering voice. Then the voice continues, "Oh no, what happened to your makeup? Tell you what, why don't you put it back on your face? It reminded me of my wife when she was younger." Martha stops pacing. Next, she uses toilet tissue papers to wipe her tears and runny makeup away. Starting from the beginning, she then puts on her makeup in front of the mirror.

"Yes, now that's just so sexy, so divinely glorious. You're giving me a hard-on, don't stop, that's it, do it for daddy. My love, paint that pretty face pretty for me, Martha," sneers the whispering voice.

On the other side of the door, the crew keeps banging, pushing, and screaming Martha's name, asking how she's holding up. Martha responds in a calm, reassuring voice, "I am hanging in there. Don't worry. I'm not going to panic, guys." The room starts getting unusually cold as ice forms on the bathroom faucet and sink.

Brandon and James pull out their axes. *Bam, bam, bam, bam.* After the fourth attempt to break the door down, the axes break off their handles, flying into the air and boomeranging back toward the group, which causes the group to run from the restroom door.

Martha stays focused. Listening to the whispering voice give her more compliments, she hopes her beauty session in front of the mirror will pay off in exchange for her freedom. Shivering from the cold, she now starts painting her nails red, shaking, and pretending as if nothing is wrong.

Outside the door, all is quiet. In a soft voice, Martha calls, "Guys, anybody out there? I'm almost done. I decided to refresh my makeup since the commotion has died down…" says Maratha gulping down the fear.

Neither side can hear the other as Alex and his crew continue screaming, pushing, kicking the bathroom door. Yet, there is still no response. Alex, Marie, Brandon, or James hear nothing.

Martha blows her nails dry. She looks in the mirror and arranges her hair. Then she pouts her lips, forming an imaginary kiss in the air. The room gets colder.

Marie and the boys outside keep screaming, banging on the door, but no sound reaches them, nothing from the inside of the restroom. Inside the restroom, Martha swallows. She licks her now white-dry cracking chapped lips, holding on to the icy porcelain sink with one hand while tracing her lips with the other. Her eardrums pop from a cracking noise coming from the mirror. She firmly grips one side of the sink, moving her other hand and wiping away the tears. When Maratha tries removing her hand from the sink, she realizes it's stuck. Looking at her hand, she tries again. She takes her free hand and tries to separate the stuck hand, but all in vain. She looks up at the mirror and finds it fogged. As she wipes it away, her eyes blink, and she kind of sees something in the mirror. Unable to comprehend what it is, she grabs more paper towels and frantically tries to wipe the mirror clean, hoping for a clear view.

Martha's eyes slowly move around to the sound. She feels something even within the mirror as she wipes it clean. Her stuck hand finally comes free. Looking at her hand, she screams out in pain, seeing it covered like a bloody hand icicle. It gets bloodier with each passing second. She realizes that white porcelain specs are embedded in her skin. Moving slowly in a complete 360-degree circle with arms to her side and hands pointing outward, she still can't make out what's in the mirror. She moves forward, taking a closer look into the mirror. Then a weird glimpse shakes her to the core. The small hairs on the back of her neck stick up like pine needles.

Before Martha could react, a dark ghostly male figure appears on the opposite side of her mirror. His dark hands, arms, and partial torso reach through the glass mirror, grab her head, and kiss and lick Martha's makeup off with his bloodied-red tongue. Martha spits in the direction of the shadowy ghost face, kicking and screaming for help continuously. The ghost then pulls her hair.

Alex and his friends now hear Martha's terrifying death screams. Brandon tries using his large football body-frame, slamming the door several times. While pounding on the door, he breaks a bone in his arm and falls to the floor, screaming in pain.

Martha tries pulling the ghost's partially visible hands away from her hair, screaming as small hair strands start separating from the side of her scalp. But the ghost refuses to let her go. The ghostly apparition keeps pulling her closer and closer to the glass mirror, her body dangling across the sink. Pressing her face on the mirror forcefully, it cracks, and tiny chips of glass fly in the air. Most of the pieces pierce the skin on Martha's face, and from a distance, they look like specks of glitter. He slowly pulls her through the mirror, slicing the sides of her face. Martha continues trying to pull her body back while holding on to the sink.

"Come to me, my love. I want you in my universe," whispers the ghost.

Alex, along with his crew, hears all this. They hear the ghost's sick-talk to Martha, her screaming for her life, and glass breaking. Trying everything from throwing school desks and chairs to using axes, the teenagers realize that nothing will help them change the situation that they are in. They hear Martha's face slowly crack against the restroom mirror painfully, bit by bit. The ghost's large, dark hand pulls Martha's face and neck with all his might. The glass sticks to her skin, piercing her wide-open eyes, her forehead, and throat.

Martha screams for her life. The ghost releases her neck, and her face falls hard on the sink, breaking the top row of her teeth. One by one, the teeth fall into the bloody sink. Blood drips from the side of her face while broken teeth float in the bloody sink. The ghost never lets go of her long hair. She is still breathing, gasping for air as he rips her hair from the scalp, pulling it back through the now almost mirrorless hole in the wall. He smashes her face powerfully into the glass, breaking big pieces of glass into tiny grains. Then the ghost repeats the process. He keeps smashing her face into the broken glass pieces, causing portions of her flesh to fall onto the floor.

Blood and tiny slices of flesh gradually run underneath the bathroom door. Alex, Brandon, James, and Marie step away from the door in total horror. Banging and screaming continuously with immense fear in their hearts, they feel helpless. The scene chills up their spines. The ground beneath their feet begins to shake. With everyone screaming, Martha's face smashes through the mirror several times. They all cry, scream, and pray outside for Maratha's suffering to stop. Then, the screaming stops. They hear skin being cut by glass as it slits her throat, finally releasing her hair, dropping her body on the restroom floor.

Alex and his friends finally bust into the restroom, and the moment they enter, they see blood everywhere. Alex rushes toward his friend. He tries to stop the massive bleeding as she takes her last breath in Alex's arms. They are all on their knees, screaming and crying, wanting this nightmare to stop.

Sadly, they did whatever was in their control, but each one of their efforts turned out to be useless. There was nothing they could do except watch Martha roll around helplessly and bleed out till her body just goes motionless. They were all in shock. They had just watched someone they knew bleed out in front of them. No words could do justice in describing how they felt at that moment.

They all look at Martha one last time, half of her face shredded up, the other half wasn't even recognizable. They look around the bathroom and see that there's blood everywhere, especially from the mirror. Even the sink is filled with a pool of blood. Glass is shattered all over the floor. Brandon points at a bloody half piece of Martha's ear floating in the blood bath.

As they were busy examining the area, something clicks Alex's mind—Crystal's absence. He runs over to James, grabs him by his shoulder to get his attention, and then says, "James, you never told us how you and Crystal got separated from each other, you guys were literally inseparable! Did you panic or forgot about her, thinking only to save your ass in a moment of fear? She was such a smart, tough girl, dammit." James looks at Alex; sadness spread all over his countenance. He doesn't know how to get the words out. Alex, who sees James hesitate, figures out what could possibly have happened. Finally, James shrugs his shoulders. Then he looks around and blurts out, "Crystal's dead."

Still shocked, Alex, Marie, Brandon, and James look outside. They notice the dark ghostly image taking out two trash bags toward the school dumpster, one large and the second relatively smaller garbage bag.

CHAPTER 8

The Ghost's Wife

READING ABOUT THE AWFUL DEATH OF POOR MARTHA makes me sick to my stomach. After hours of reading, I finally decide to put down this morbid diary book, thinking, *What kind of a sick person even thinks like this?*

In an attempt to forget about the events that I'd read in the book about Alex and his friends trapped in the high school, I decided to take a little rest and turn in for the night, thinking my mind deserves it. I take a shower, grab the newspaper, and climbing into bed, I hit the remote. As soon as the television opens, a news channel announces, "Authorities are still looking for a missing teen last reportedly seen entering Palmyra High school." I hoop out of bed at once, put on my robe and slippers, and run downstairs to get the composition book, only to find that it's not where I had put it earlier. "Damn it, not again! Why the hell does this book keep disappearing!"

I call for Chester in the house and then outside, but just like the composition book, he's nowhere to be found. Unbeknown to me, Chester runs down the moon-lit street toward Ariel and Biff's partially burnt house with the book in his mouth. He does his usual routine, leaps four feet into the open bedroom window and places the book onto the bedroom desk. The wooden floor loudly squeaks as a tall, dark shadowy figure walks past the bedroom doorway. A cold breeze blows the bedroom curtains. That's when the pointed-ear short-tail red Doberman leaps out of the window and sprints some three miles back to my estate. It is only when he hurdles over my house's iron-rod fence, clearing six feet to the grounds, that I meet him. Immediately, Chester submits, going to the ground, crawling. With his head down, he whimpers as if to ask for forgiveness.

"Where were you, Chester? I had been looking for you everywhere," I ask him while gently rubbing his head. After that, we both head back to the house.

* * *

It's Saturday afternoon, and Ariel goes back to her burnt house with a contractor after deciding she is going to restore the home Biff had built for their family.

"Why don't we just let the insurance company fix the fire damage and sell the place, Ariel?" says the contractor, Bob, a friend of the family.

"No. Biff and I had built this place together. It has memories that can't be erased that easily. Besides, I can feel his presence every time I enter the house. It's like he's trying to still come home," says Ariel. She goes over the blueprints for restoring her house. Ariel leaves Bob and walks back into her partially burned bedroom. She picks up the composition book sitting on her and her late husband's desk. Then she begins reading Biff's diary, his life's story up to the horrific accounts of different events taking place at her husband's former place of business—the Palmyra High School. She also reads about her birth town—a city where they had raised a family—and is moved every time he calls her "Sunshine."

Tears stream down Ariel's eyes as she sits down, thumbing through the book, occasionally running her finger across the red writings while weeping and trembling. After reading about Crystal's tragic death, she reads about the torture and terrorizing of Martha, a young high school senior who was hit repeatedly on a glass bathroom mirror. While learning of her late husband's orgasmic rush to confront fear, Ariel's mobile phone rings, breaking her deep concentration. The book falls from her hand and drops on the floor. Startled, Ariel answers the call, which is from her daughter. "This is Amy, Jack, and Biff Jr are coming with me over to the house. Wait for us," says Amy.

A dark cloud loom in the sky, winds pick up, and a heavy rainstorm dominates the neighborhood as the triplet brothers and sister arrive down the rainy street in a red Ford Super DF-450 Platinum truck. After running inside, they call the house for their mom. Ariel is found in the bedroom, listening intently to the sound of water dripping from the house's ceiling into plastic trash containers throughout the house.

"Mom, let's come back tomorrow with the contractors. People from the roofing company will come to repair the roof. Till then, let's go back to the hotel suite," says Biff Jr.

Amy, in the meantime, notices the book on their bedroom desk. She picks it up and begins skimming through it. "Mom, what's this?" asks Amy. Everyone in the bedroom starts looking at Amy's expression as she grabs her face in shock and awe, asking what's wrong. "Mom, this looks like a diary from dad. I mean, after he writes about you guys... I don't understand... all this, in red. I can't figure it out. What's going on, mom? With this horrible writing in red...Why is this mixed together?" stammers Amy while bombarding her mother with broken sentences. Ariel calmly pulls the book out of her daughter's hands and places it on the desk. Signaling her children to leave her room, she says, "Why don't you all go out for dinner and come back tomorrow?"

* * *

The next day not a single cloud was to be seen in the sky as Ariel, and her triplets pull up to meet the roofing company and their general contractor. During loud hammering of a new roof, the contractor goes over the new architectural plans. Ariel says to the contractor, "Only replace the roof and floors in my and Biff's master-size bedroom. Other than that, leave the room as is. Do not remove any furniture that may be burnt. Do not even replace the burnt edges of the window. Also, do not replace the staining wood. Leave things the way they are."

At that moment, Amy speaks up, "Mom, you sure about this? We must replace everything or just move out."

"No, children. That won't happen," replies Ariel somberly.

Then Ariel shows her kids the plans for a new master addition on the opposite side of the house. Biff Jr. walks into the old room while others are walking around the property.

"Hey, has anybody seen dad's diary, the black composition book?" asks Biff Jr.

Ariel walks into the bedroom, telling her kids not to worry about it, as it's not lost. After walking and talking for hours with the contractor, the family leaves for a steak dinner. Ariel explains her theory of their dad being dead but not entirely dead. She says to them, "I think your father's spirit is involved in the live, real-time hauntings at the school that is happening these days."

Ariel's kids still think their mother should just fix up the house, rent it out, or perhaps sell the property altogether. They want to just leave their past behind, move to Las Vegas, and spend more time with the grandkids. They all wish to start a new life as soon as possible and let their father's spirit figure out how to get out of purgatory.

Ariel insists, "No, I must stay and help put my husband, your loving dad's soul, to rest so he can get out of purgatory. Children, there is still hope for your dad. I have a plan to help restore his soul and send it to its peaceful resting place." Then Ariel tries to explain further, saying to them, "While your dad's confessed writings in his composition book are horrible, the Bible says, 'purgatory is temporary' because your dad died in God's friendship. There is still hope for him, and I must stay by his side."

After a pause, she continues, "He lived a God-fearing life; he will have eternal salvation." Then she adds, "Your dad's spirit needs purification in order to enter heaven. We need time," she pleads. "We need to pray for his soul to be restored."

They leave the house arriving at the Palmyra Catholic Cathedral. It's early evening, and Ariel prearranges a meeting for her family to speak with Bishop Faye in the main cathedral. He explains their loved one's situation, telling them their dead fathers' spirit is a vengeful spirit—one that only wants to make others suffer. Anyone entering after sundown, where he died accidentally, should pay for taking him away from the love of his life—Ariel. This is how the vengeful spirit feels.

Suddenly, the large cathedral starts swaying side to side; the family members look at one another in shock. "Remain calm. Let us join hands and bow our heads, for God so loved the world that he gave is only so that whosoever perish shall have everlasting life," after a brief pause, Bishop Faye says, "Jesus, Jesus."

The building stops swaying as the family looks around. Bishop Faye goes on to explain the importance of praying for Biff because the Catechism says, "The imperfectly purified soul still has a chance for eternal salvation." He reminds them their loved ones must stop thinking about his personal pain, for if he would take the pain to heaven, he will eternally be miserable in heaven.

"If your husband, your dad is to live in eternity with God, he needs healing, his soul, his spirit must make amends," says Bishop Faye. Telling them they must become selfless and maintain vigilance. Going through a purification prayer, holy communion, wearing holy Rosary Beads, and faith will help save Biff from eternal hell and damnation. The Bishop ends by saying once Biff undergoes purification, he will have the holiness he needs to enter the joy of heaven.

CHAPTER 9

Trapped in School

EVERYONE'S JAWS DROP IN RESPONSE TO JAMES' AWFUL account of Crystal's tragic death. Alex was upset and, to some extent, even furious to know that two of his crew members were murdered all because of a bunch of missing keys and the possible kidnapping of Amelio created by the paranormal actions of a dead janitor.

After a brief silence, Alex says to his friends, "I believe this ghost is trying to pick us off one by one until each one of us is dead." James, Brandon, and Marie feel the same but are too afraid to say anything. They sense danger, their throats dry, they're thirsty beyond words. Mentally drained, their bodies are starting to wear down from the shock of never-ending drama and uncertainty.

"This ghost ain't playing around. We've got to recalibrate and stick to our plan," continues Alex.

"Leave us the hell alone, we just want to go home! Can you please stop it?" cries Marie in exasperation. She completely loses it, screaming at the top of her lungs until she becomes exhausted. Lights flicker on and off in the hallway, and heavy rains begin to pour on the school's rooftop. Brandon paces back and forth with hands on his head, pulling his hair and grunting out of frustration. Still mourning over the death of his girlfriend, James crouches on his knees. His hands cover his face, and he keeps crying his eyes out in sorrow.

Alex slowly looks around the room at everyone one by one. Watching his friends, he feels great pangs of regret, wishing he'd just come alone. *We're all teenagers. We should be out there, enjoying our spring break, not experiencing senseless deaths of our classmates,* thinks Alex to himself as gloominess spreads over his countenance.

Just then, Brandon walks up to Alex. He pulls him to the side and says, "We need to get out of the school, Alex. After losing Crystal and Martha, our chances of finding Amelio being alive are very slim. Accept it, dude. It's time to save ourselves."

"Guys, I'm sorry for putting you all in this awful situation. We're in the ghost's playground and need a new plan of escape," Alex tells them. Then he continues, "We must stick together. No matter what befalls, everyone watches everybody's back. Understood?" They all nod quietly. Brandon grabs coats from a nearby classroom. As he hands them to his friends, they walk over to Martha's body, each dropping a coat in an attempt to cover her body.

Running in a tight pack, they see the original window Martha busted open with a rock when they first entered the school. The window insight gives them new, unexplainable energy, hope, and happiness. With smiles on their faces, their pace gets faster, running toward the window. Overhead, the lights continue to fluctuate as rain clouds color the sky black. Looking side to side now sprinting, Brandon and James run in the rear. Then running forward, turning around, running backward, and then pedaling forward again, the group does not come across any eerie presence. With no ghost or any gagging odors, they feel surprisingly good for getting so close to the exit.

We'll finally be out of this shit place, thinks Alex.

The smell of rain enters their nostrils, and they are aware of the fact that they're getting closer to being outside. They hope this "monster" will stay away long enough for them to escape the building. Halfway to the window, they see broken glass on the floor.

Seconds later, a large dark human silhouette walks above the glass while pushing a mop bucket. It keeps going. They begin to wonder if he noticed them. Quietly, they run to a nearby side in the hallway. Bending over with hands on their knees, they sweat from head to toe. They try to catch their breaths. Then their eyes scan around, not noticing or hearing any strange noises. Slowly, they tip-toe toward the window.

Almost there..., thinks Alex. On the floor, they see the broken glass and the rock that Martha had hit earlier. A strange, cold, rainy-air mist hits their faces.

When Alex walks up to the window, he realizes it's not broken. Although there are pieces of broken glass everywhere, the window itself looks brand-new. Brandon motions for everyone else to move to one side of the window. He picks up the rock from the floor. Then using all the weight from his large launches, he throws the rock into the glass at what looks like 80-miles-per-hour speed. Surprisingly, the rock bounces off. It comes back toward Brandon, knocking him to the floor on top of the broken glass that had been scattered all over the floor ever since Martha had hit the window. In an attempt to get up, he slips on large glass pieces that cut his hands. They pierce his face and several other portions of his torso.

"Who fixed the window?" asks Marie in a trembling voice.

"Nobody but the freaking janitor. Show yourself, bastard! Get some freaking balls because when you do, I'm gonna send you straight to hell!" says James. In anger, he picks up the rock and throws it at the window.

They all watch, astounded, as the rock explodes into a million tiny, pointy chips of pebbles. They quickly put hands over their faces and fall to the ground as pieces of rock rain down on them, pounding their skin, hitting their necks, and landing in their hair. Lights flickering in a strobe continue to flash on and off. Then suddenly, the temperature drops. Soon after that, the sound of janitor's keys jiggling starts echoing throughout the building. "Ha, ha, ha, ha!" A burst of loud laughter, whistling in the cadence of his giggling keys, follows.

Putting his index finger on his lips, Alex signals everyone to stay silent. They listen but are met with silence. But then, loud laughter erupts again, sending chills through their bodies. Alex, James, Brandon, and Marie look at one another with fear in their eyes, feeling the ghost's presence getting even closer. After a few seconds, Alex whispers, "Follow me."

They tiptoe down the hallway. With each step, they feel the air getting colder. Shivering and rubbing their hands together while blowing in them, they pass classrooms. When they drop their heads, the smell of something worse than a dead skunk hits their nose. Alex swallows his own vomit, trying to keep the noise down. One by one, the doors open. With each classroom they walk past down the hallway, Brandon and James cover Alex and Marie's back. They continue looking, protecting them from behind as Alex and Marie move to find a new exit window.

While still wandering, Marie looks above her head and sees a dark shadow at the ceiling, getting bigger and bigger. The shadow starts walking toward them. "Oh my god!" she screams before putting her hand over her mouth. Everyone stops in their tracks. Then looking up and breathing heavily, they watch the shadow move on the ceiling. Panicked, they turn around to look who's present but are shocked to see no one behind them. They hear heavy footsteps stomping louder and heavier as if a large rhino or elephant was after them. The sound is so loud and rumbling they feel it coming in their direction.

Sensing more urgencies, everyone sprints to the nearest double doors. They slam and lock them shut. But the snarling animal sounds follow. It gets closer to them. Then *bam, boom,* their heavy metal double doors start shaking. Soon, they hear claw-like feet walk away from the door. But only seconds later, they hear the feet clicking on the other side of the door. The creature runs toward their doors, slamming its body into them, perhaps like a bull, laughing as if he is toying with them. Alex, James, Brandon, and Marie pull down a large metal pole onto the door brace, hoping to stop the beast's entry.

The ghost keeps ramming into the doors, going crazy. He refuses to give up. After trying constantly, he manages to crack a wedge open. The opening is large enough for him to put his arm through the door. The group remains crouched in front of it, thinking their body weight will help keep the double doors secure.

In a blink of an eye, a long black arm comes through the wedge with extremely long fingers. The hand grabs James by the wrist, pulling his hand and wrist through the wedge, brutally crushing his wrist. James fights, and Brandon pulls on James' legs, but all in vain. James screams for help, but the ghost refuses to let go of his wrist. He keeps pulling James' arm through the wedge. That's when Alex hears James' bones crack as his arm is forced through the wedge. James' arm snaps at the elbow.

On the other side of the door, the ghost stands in front of the double metal doors, holding the front portion of James' bloodied hand and arm in his hand. Racing back through the wedge, his long dark, bloody arm and hands reach for James. Alex, Brandon, and Marie drag James' body away from the door. Alex reaches into his pocket to take out his mace spray. He switches the blade, aiming it at his flopping, searching arm, and sends the knife deep into his par-tially-visible hand. The arm movement stops. He shakes the knife from his hand. Everything is silent for a while as they watch his arm pull away through the wedge away from them as sunlight peers through the wedge.

By this time, James is on the floor. He cries his eyes out in pain because of the ghost crushing his upper left arm down to the elbow. Brandon and Alex take off their shirts. They all strip down using their undergarments as well to help stop the bleeding. Then they get dressed again. Marie, in the meantime, applies a tourniquet because of which James screams out in excruciating pain. His shrieks bounce off the school lockers. A dark human-like body roars like a lion down the halls, ripping the lockers out of the wall. Then abruptly, the ghost stops. It sounds like he has left. Soon, it gets surprisingly quiet.

While Marie tends to James, Alex and Brandon get their ears to the door, peeping through the wedge. They don't hear nor see him. Then Alex says to Brandon, "Dude, crack open the door. Double check for a clear sign to escape this room."

James looks back at Alex with a crazy look on his face and, in a deep whisper, shoots back, "No! Stay put! Please don't open the door, at least not right now."

Few seconds pass by, then Alex says to Brandon, "Brother, you need to step aside. Hurry up, move aside." Alex feels he can peek out the wedge and try to open the door, but it won't budge. "Double doors locked! Great, now we're really screwed. Stuck in this maintenance room with no windows or alternative doors. No way out... Period," says Alex, frustrated and equally scared. Everything seems to be falling apart for Alex and his group. Helpless and drained out, they all feel trapped. After a few silent seconds, Alex speaks up again, "So basically, the ghost just set us up to get us where he wants us to be—stuck with nowhere to go in this room." James begins to weep uncontrollably, more due to the fear of the unknown and less because of the pain that he was experiencing.

Alex, too, completely feels lost. He walks to the corner of the room, sits on the floor, and drops his head in his hands. Brandon and Marie continue nursing James' bleeding elbow, trying to keep it elevated. They begin consoling him, trying to keep his mind off his pain.

At that moment, words were not needed to express how each one of them felt. Their facial expressions were enough to communicate their unexplainable feelings of misery, hopelessness, and fear. Lost at this moment in time. Sitting hopelessly, they know they need nothing short of a miracle to happen. That's because they know the ghost of Biff, the janitor, is plotting his next move. He will come back for his killing spree shortly.

"Alex, before we got here, you mentioned you did some research on this place being haunted. What happened?" Marie asks Alex.

"Well, long story short, it is known that a school janitor died in this building supposedly from a heart attack in his janitor's closet," Alex tells Marie. He continues, "The police report says they found firecrackers and M-80 firecracker gunpowder near the closet. They think some high school kids got into the building one night. They played some kind of a prank that resulted in his death. Since they could never prove who the kids were, the case was ruled death by a heart attack."

"You think that guy's spirit is haunting us?" asks Brandon.

"Honestly, I don't believe in ghosts, but I do think that something or someone really psycho is out here to kill us," responds Alex.

Then an idea pops into Alex's brain. He remembers that there's an elevator on the third floor. Alex jumps up and clapping his hands quickly with excitement, tells everyone what to do next. "Guys, if we open the electrical closet in this maintenance room, there is a ventilation space. If we crawl through it, it'll lead us to the third floor directing us back to the main hallway to an emergency exit door where the alarm system is connected to the police and fire station."

Although they all are still scared, at this point, since they have nothing to lose, they think of giving it a shot.

Brandon and Alex take a large crowbar and open the huge metal vent, separating it from the utility wall. It's large enough for the four of them, but only if they tightly squeeze their bodies and crawl on their stomachs. Using their elbows and knees to crawl some 15 yards to another vent, they begin their journey. James begins moaning and groaning, leaving a trail of blood along the way behind them. As Brandon pulls him, James bites his tongue so hard blood is filling his mouth, causing him to spit and cough.

Finally, they are at the vent. Alex kicks several times with all the strength he has. Marie, too, tries to help, but they can't get it open. Brandon leaves James and manages to squeeze his large frame over

Alex and Marie's bodies, successfully kicking the vent covering out. All four of them crawl out at the corner of the third-floor hallway.

They start to walk past where Martha was killed. The closer they go down the hallway, they get confused because her body is no longer where she had died. All the blood that had spread across the floor, the clothes that they had used to cover Martha's body, no longer there. But without wasting any of their time, they resume moving. "Don't know why he took her body. But, well, it kind of makes sense. He was an old janitor, so maybe he's just cleaning up after himself or something. Who knows what the ghost is doing with the bodies?" says Alex thoughtfully while moving forward.

James begins wondering if his girl Crystal's body is still in the school. *Most likely, the ghost cleaned up that too,* thinks James.

Walking slowly, the group finally reaches the principal's office. This is from where they had tried to escape the first time Alex was here, and the lock broke. *So, this is a go,* thinks Alex. A little way up, they're getting close to the third floor. They are unable to see anything, as it is pitch black dark around the corner of the hallway. The air starts getting cold, and a small breeze flows through the air. They get closer to the edge of the hallway. That's when Alex signals for everyone to pause at the halfway point. He tells them he'll take a quick peek just in case the shadow figure is waiting around the corner.

Alex gets on all fours, crawling and getting closer to the elevator. He looks to both sides of his body, but the halls look empty. He signals his friends to move toward him with the same low crawl. The area is clear, but the halls are ice cold to the extent that the locker starts getting frost on them. Every time they exhale, a frail cloud of smoke escapes their mouth. Alex begins shivering, not knowing whether it is due to cold or fear.

On their way to the elevator, the repulsive smell comes back. Around the corner, getting closer to the elevator, the group decides not to give up. They remain determined in their tracks. In the background, James starts complaining that his upper arm is getting numb.

"It's starting to turn green," complains James. Then asks Marie, "Can you wrap it tighter?"

Alex speaks up, "James, please hold up. Wait till we get to the elevator." James shakes his head in agreement. The group feels the ghost's presence again. They realize that every time they smell the odor of dead bodies or flesh, he's nearby.

They move quickly, but at this moment, Alex feels sick to his stomach like he knows something is going to go down any moment. *Hope I'm wrong,* thinks Alex to himself. As they get to the elevator, Alex repeatedly punches the button, stomping his feet, but there is no movement. "Damn, guys, the electric power is off in the building," Alex reminds everybody while standing near the elevator.

Then Alex takes a moment to gather his thoughts. Signaling Marie to re-bandage James' arm, he looks for a way to manually open the elevator doors. Marie reaches out near Alex as he's turning toward the hallway's corner. She puts her hand in the back of his pants near his butt crack, pulling him backward. Alex falls on his back. Then she reaches in her backpack, pulls out the crowbar, and puts it in his hand, motioning him toward the elevator doors. Alex takes the metal pipe. Slowly opening it, he asks Brandon to grab the door the moment he props it open. Alex grabs his side, and they both pull, splitting the doors open.

The elevator is all the way at the bottom. Alex can't really tell, but it looks like it goes past the first floor to the basement. *I didn't know this school had a basement. Whatever, the basement is better than nothing at all,* thinks Alex.

Marie finishes wrapping James' arm. Signaling he feels better, she gives Alex and Brandon the thumbs-up sign. Now the real question is, who's going to go down the elevator shaft first? Looking down, Alex sees a combination of eight long, thick ropes and chains connected to the elevators. The pulley wheels and axle used move the elevator up and down. All this looks serious. Alex says, "Guys, we have to be quick and careful." Then James asks, "How am I going to get down. I just have one hand. Remember?"

"You're right, James, there's no way you can climb down," Alex tells James.

"If there is an electrical closet in the basement, there has to be a fuse box to restore power to the building," says Brandon.

"Guys, guys, it's obvious," speaks up James. "If I slip, I'll slam to my death, probably snapping my neck. I have to stay, give the three of you the chance to get out."

"No, no, we're in this together. We've been through too much together. Look at yourself," says Marie.

The death odor gets closer, and keys start jiggling. Alex looks at Marie and Brandon and asks, "Who's going down first?"

Since the boys had used their top undergarments earlier while covering Martha's disfigured mutilated body, it was Marie's time to sacrifice this time. She takes off her bra. Next, she grips one thick rope and, using her bra, slides down to the bottom, screaming, "Oh my god, my hands are starting to burn," screams Marie. *Bam.* "Guys, I think the rope burned through some of my bra. Try hugging the rope more with your body," says Marie.

Brandon is next. He takes off his pants and slides down, "I'm here! Guys, come on, use the chain it's smoother, not as painful as the rope," says Brandon.

Around the corner behind James and Alex, heavy footsteps start stomping closer. They look up at the ceiling and watch the ghostly figure move closer toward them. Alex tries one more time encouraging James to go for it, but he refuses to listen to Alex, insisting he's going to stay behind. "Alex, I just lost my Crystal. Me going down is too risky. If this thing kills me, my spirit will never stop fighting him. I'll do my best to avenge my Crystal's death. Now go, he's getting closer," says James. He picks up the metal pipe with his good hand and arm. Sees the ghost walking toward him, the keys jingling. "Go, my friend, go now," says James. Footsteps getting louder, shaking the floor, Alex takes off his pants. Then he jumps, grabs the metal chain with his pants, and slides down to the bottom of the elevator top.

The moment Alex lands, Marie asks about James. "He decided to sacrifice his life and buy us some time," replies Alex. Standing at the top of the elevator, looking up, they listen to the loud stomps, elevator shaft ropes, and chains swaying back and forth. They notice the emergency door exit, and so they jump through it onto the elevator floor.

They stand below, listening to the loud noises happening on the third floor to James.

Above, James stands face to face with the ghost as the 6'3" ghost looks down on James' 5'10" frame, scared out of his mind. He's ready to fight for his Crystal. The tall figure's large head with glowing large monster eyes, dark head, and torso lingers. The mid-section of his body, exposing muscle and white legs, rapidly approach.

James, staring directly at the ghost, holds his metal rod tightly with tears in his eyes. He lunges his body toward the ghost taking a swing, hitting him in the face. The ghost wipes his face. James takes a 360-degree turn and lunges again, hitting the ghost. The ghost stands there with a white glow around his body. Then he grabs James by the neck. James starts kicking and screaming. He swings the crowbar near the ghost's head. Looking directly at James' face, he smiles. While James' feet dangle in the air kicking, urine oozes through his jeans, down his legs into his socks, soaking his canvas sneakers. James keeps trying to strike the ghost in the head, but the ghost keeps narrowly missing. Furious, the ghost yanks the crowbar from his hand, now beating James on his half arm, causing blood to gush like a showerhead. Alex, Marie, and Brandon hear and feel every blow peeping through the elevator hatch door. Marie slides down to the floor with hands over her ears.

Once the ghost is done beating James with the crowbar, he holds him by his neck.

Alex, Marie, and Brandon see that James is still alive; his face is in the direction of the elevator emergency door. The ghost walks closer to the edge of the elevator, holding a kicking, bleeding, and screaming James over the edge. Then he lets go of James. His friends whimper as they watch James fall to his death. His battered head slams through the top emergency door exit, sending blood and flesh all inside the elevator space. His head rolls over to Marie's crouched position, sending her into hysteria. She screams and cries uncontrollably.

The ghost's heavy footsteps shake the building, walking away from the elevator down the school hallway into a classroom.

CHAPTER 10

The Professor's Search for Truth

AS THE DARK NIGHT CREEPS IN WITH HARDLY ANY STARS visible in the sky, cool winds begin blowing around 2:00 a.m. The next day, on Saturday morning, strong winds howl against the third-floor windowpane at Palmyra High School, where Biff's dark, ghostly figure is busy writing in blood. Engrossed in writing, he narrates his latest and most gruesome, vengeful encounter with the teenagers. With a wicked grin on his ghostly countenance, he writes about frightening and frustrating the shit out of the group who loitered around in pursuit of finding Amelio, who is yet to be found.

Alex and the remaining members of his group believe Amelio is still alive, perhaps hidden away from the ghostly hands of Biff's evil spirit. Several hours tick away, but no one gives up on their search of their friend Amelio—an innocent well-wisher who just wished to help Alex find his keys and nothing more. After wandering across the building some more, Alex loses hope in finding his friend. He suggests to the group they leave the ghost alone and try to just stay alive and leave Amelio's disappearance in the hands of the law enforcement agencies. After hours of struggle and pain, and tears, the group finally decides to find an exit and leave the premises. Biff's dark ghostly figure walks outside the school onto the school's football field. Sitting on the ground, his attention is caught by a tall, dark, mysterious figure approaching him. On a closer look, he realizes it's Chester, the Doberman. Chester takes the composition book from the dark ghostly hand and runs off like a racer through a wooded area.

* * *

Early on Sunday morning, I open the front door of my home, intending on starting my morning jog. But the moment I step out, I trip over the same black composition diary, lying on the floor on the entrance mat. When I look closely at this book, I see that it is wet with red droppings again. I can't figure out if it is paint, or something else, hoping it's not what I think it is—blood. Whatever the situation, it has got me more curious now. The book reeks a peculiar, stomach-churning odor that makes me want to vomit. I go back to the house, get gloves, a mask, goggles, and a plastic bag. Instead of reading this composition diary in my house, I decided to read it in my work shed while standing up. As I turn the pages, reading whatever is written in red ink, my heart races. It races because the red droppings on the pages don't look like ink. After reading the latest detailed encounter where this ghost sent an axe through a closet door, killing a girl with the group, I had to believe that there is a connection between Biff, the Palmyra High School's deceased janitor from a year ago, and these weird writings.

While reading the book, my thought processes become more bizarre and harder to comprehend. *Is there some connection between these strange writings of this book, my dog disappearing, and my house and mind being haunted every time I read the diary?*

I continue wondering if it is at all possible that this man's dead spirit is haunting and killing folks that come in the building after dark. That's when I decide to stop by *The Chronicle*, the local newspaper's office, and do some research on the school on my own.

The next morning, on Monday, I walk into the office, and as soon as I get to the reception desk, I ask: "Is the publisher available?"

After asking me who I am, the receptionist tells the person on the phone my identity. Then she says, "Please have a seat. Someone will get in touch with you shortly."

Soon a lady comes to greet me and introduces herself as Ariel. Then she walks me back to her office.

As we both sit in her room, I ask her if she has any news clippings or reports regarding the janitor who died at the local school. A weird sadness spreads over her face. But then, unwinding herself, she picks up the phone and asks someone to bring copies of newspaper clippings of Palmyra High School about the janitor. At this point, I had no clue that Ariel was asking her co-worker to provide me with information on her dead husband.

A young high school-age girl brings me a folder. Ariel stands up and gives me a cold look. Her head slightly bent down and looking over the top of her white glasses, she says, "Well, sir, I hope this helps. Give us a call if you need anything more. Have a good day, sir." Ariel was direct, firm, and matter-of-fact.

After thanking her and saying goodbye, I walk to my car and reach for my keys, only to find out that they are not in my pocket. "That's odd." Thinking that I must have left them in the newspaper office, I walk back. As I turn the doorknob, it won't budge. I knock on the door, peering in the window, "Hello? There? Can you see me? The door won't open. I think my keys are inside your office," I announce. But no response. The receptionist acts as though I am invisible. "This makes no sense."

Disappointed, I walk back to my car and, surprisingly, see that the keys are in the door. I open the door and feel a cold, wintry breeze hit my face. I rush in to start the car, but before I could do anything, the doors automatically shut and lock, and a black cloud of smoke overwhelm my car. With the car doors locked, I begin screaming and blowing the horn, but no one responds from the outside. Seconds later, the car starts up on its own. As I continue panicking, the windows come down, and much to my relief, the doors unlock. Now I'm really pissed and absolutely determined to find out the truth.

As soon as I get home, I take a deep dive into the clippings and start researching online. Then stopping midway, I go to my tool shed, planning on taking the black diary before I resume my research session. As I walk in, I see that the book was nowhere to be found.

During this time, unbeknownst to me, Chester leaps inside Ariel's remodeled bedroom window, which is always mysteriously left open. As the sun sets, Chester drops the book on the bedroom desk and leaps out of the window, racing home. At this point, Ariel's home is fully in the process of being remodeled. She purposely tries to keep as much of the original master room intact as she can.

One late night, around 11 p.m., Ariel walks into the partially remodeled house with new floors and partially burnt walls. Ariel hears a noise in her old master bedroom. She walks into her kitchen, opens the door of her wine collection, and, after pulling out a bottle of Marcassin Chardonnay Vineyard 2009, pops the top. She walks into the old master bedroom and spots the composition book on the table. With bottle and glass in hand, she sits down and lights a huge candle. Occasionally sipping from her wine glass, she spends the next few hours reading her dead husband's memoirs, chronicling from beginning to after his death.

When Ariel finishes reading the composition book, she pulls out her cell phone and demands all three triplets to visit that evening. Simultaneously, her triplets arrive at the house at the same time.

"Children, there's a reason why I called you all today," says Ariel. Then she continues, "The plan for the evening is to call up your father because I believe, and rightly so, that his spirit is involved in vengeful deeds, taking the lives of innocent young people at the school."

When the three children nod in agreement, Ariel goes down a list of items necessary to conduct their séance. An oval table is carried into a vacant room in the house. Then a small lamp, a glass of water, a pad of paper and a pencil. The room is cleansed as one of the triplets walks the room using a bowl of crushed orange peels, adding a drop of vanilla extract. The room is also surrounded by candles, giving off a vanilla scent in the séance room.

Once the room is ready, the family of four sits around the table. Ariel gives her three adult children instructions to close their eyes, take slow, deep breaths, telling them to relax. As the candles in their room begin flickering, Ariel tells everyone to stay calm, instructing them to place their hands on their table and connect hands. Ariel tells everyone to repeat after her chant, "Dear Biff Saw, our beloved husband and father, we ask you to please move among us. We ask for you to speak through all of us. Your family is here, welcoming your spirit with an open heart and mind. Show yourself so we can help save you from hell."

Everyone is very still. The room starts getting colder, so much so when the group speaks, frail smoke comes from their breath. Some of the family members begin to shiver. Everyone tries to listen carefully for any kind of sound that may signal that the spirit of Biff is attempting to reach them. Ariel is watching their glass of water for movements. Soon, the water inside the glass begins to make bubbly sounds as if it's boiling. Ariel asks a question, "Biff, are you in the room with us? If yes, please know that we love you. Don't be afraid," says Ariel.

There is a continued silence. Then Ariel speaks again, "Honey, we love you, we miss you. Tap twice for yes. Can you hear my voice?" says Ariel. The room gets colder, but the water in the glass is now boiling. Suddenly, the room gets warmer, and the glass filled with water freezes. It slides in front of Ariel and levitates in the air. Then it slowly goes down and taps the table twice. Still holding hands, everyone opens their eyes in amazement but not uttering a word at this point.

Suddenly, the pen on the table levitates and starts circling on the paper in front of everyone. The pen begins outlining everyone's faces and then writes on the paper: "I miss my family." After a pause, "I'm sorry I didn't make it home my Sunshine, for our special night," writes Biff's invisible spirit. Tears start streaming down his daughter's face. Even the boys' eyes tear up too. Everyone is sniffling and shaking visibly.

Then Ariel speaks up, "What's going on at the high school? What can we do to help resolve your issues?" The room turns ice cold, so much so that Jack stands up and says, "God help us!" In an instant, the candles go out, and the room gives off a skunk-like odor. Everyone gets up from the table. Amy turns on the lights. They all gasp as they see *HELP ME!* written on the table in bold red letters. Everyone in the room rubs their arms as the chill bumps and hairs stand up on their skin. The room is freezing cold. Then Biff Jr. says, "Mother, I feel the presence of something. Not sure what or who it is."

Amy says, "Yes, mom. I feel something too."

They all come closer and grip one another's hands. Tears streaming down her eyes, Amy then says with a cracking voice, "D-daddy, are you here? We want to help you, daddy. Please show your face. Say something, please."

A tall, dark, shadowy human image appears in the corner of the room with a black oily substance rolling down the room walls. The room door whistles shut. In a pitch-black room, a single light beams down on a floating body that is jet black, with no facial expressions from head to toe. Like helicopter wings, the human image spins a couple of times. With each 360 -degree turn, a loud ping sound echoes in the room. The dark shadowy figure morphs through the room ceiling, leaving a pile of ashes on the table, nearly two feet high. The room smells like burnt coals, flaking throughout the room. The ashes pour off the table on the floor, ankle-high. Everyone rushes outside the room, crying and looking around with shock, fear, and amazement.

"What's next?" asks Jack.

"Your father needs us. His soul is not settled. A demon spirit has your father..." replies Ariel. As there is no further response, everyone leaves the house, including Ariel.

Sitting next to the house, Chester takes off running after what appears to be a large, bat-like figure, flying left and right, up and down, ultimately moving forward into the starlit skies.

CHAPTER 11

Finding Amelio

STILL STUCK IN THE PALMYRA HIGH SCHOOL, BRANDON, Marie, and Alex continue to struggle. With dry throats, parched lips, tired eyes, and poignant expressions etched on their faces, it seemed as if the three hadn't slept in days.

"Our group is getting smaller and smaller. I will never get over how James sacrificed his life to save us," says Alex.

"I just hope it pays off for good. None of us ever asked for all this crap," says Brandon.

Alex looks at the other two and says, "Guys, we got to stay focused. We have to move on and find a way out of this place. Right now, I think we're in the basement of the school. Not for sure, but once we are able to get these elevator doors open, we will know our location."

Brandon and Alex try squeezing their fingers between the elevator door, but it shuts super tight. "We need something like a pipe or crowbar like we had on the third floor to force the doors open," says Brandon.

There's nothing in the elevator, nothing but a dark room, four walls, yet it feels as if someone or perhaps something is holding it from the inside. Alex gets irritated. He says, "There seems to be something in the way, stopping us from escaping."

"The only thing I can think of is hoping that the ghost dropped a pipe when he dropped James over the edge," says Alex. "The only way to find out is to go peek."

The emergency exit door was on the roof of the elevator and kind of high up. Brandon looks at Marie and asks, "Hey, will you peek if I put you on my shoulders and lift you? Can you see if that pipe fell on top of the elevator?"

"Yeah, why not! I don't care. I'll do whatever it takes for us to get out of this hell house," says Marie. Brandon positions himself, telling her to hop on his shoulders, lifting her high enough to reach the door and peek outside. Slowly, he pushes Marie up on the emergency elevator door. Pressing her nose, exposing her wondering eyes, and looking side to side, Marie says in a whisper, "It looks clear." The only thing there that she tries to ignore is James' headless body, dropped on top of the elevator shaft.

Marie vomits, puking her guts out the moment her eyes see the headless body, spitting chunks on the elevator top. Marie urges Brandon to boost her up so she can climb out of the elevator. Crawling out, Marie covers her mouth and nose, looking at James' mutilated body. The sight of James' headless body makes her drift off, blanking out for a few seconds. Alex screams Marie's name nervously after her five seconds of silence. "I'm good, I'm good," she replies.

Looking around her surroundings in the corner of the elevator, Marie spots the crowbar used to open the door from upstairs. Using the tips of her fingers, she slowly picks up the crowbar that is drowning in James' blood from the ghost's brutal head-bashing and decapitation. *Only a ghost monster has the strength to disfigure someone this way,* thinks Marie.

Carefully maneuvering the crowbar, trying not to get blood on her body, Marie walks back to the door and drops it down in front of

Brandon and Alex. As it hits the elevator floor, tiny, wet blood splatters on their faces and necks. They turn their bodies in an attempt to escape the stain of blood, but, too late. Marie jumps down right behind it, wiping blood off her partially torn bra, using the tips of her fingers. It doesn't really help; it just gets smeared all over the naked part of her upper body and breasts.

Alex picks up the bloody crowbar, so he can open the doors. He shoves the crowbar into the elevator doors, desperately trying to crack them open. Brandon grabs one side as Alex grabs the other. After getting blisters on their hands, both doors finally come apart. Cracking doors enough to wedge the crowbar between the doors, they crawl out to the basement level. The three of them sneeze as their noses take in a gross earthly smell of old mold, a thick odor heavy on their lungs. The basement is dark, with dozens of mice scattering back and forth across the floor into the even darker edges of the hallway. Their ears ring from the shattering sound of an old furnace that is trying to heat the building. Their hearts pound faster as they look at spiders crawling on webs thicker than cotton candy, moving up and down the walls. Wolf spiders, bigger than one's hands. "This is worse than upstairs," says Brandon.

They carefully move forward, cutting through spider webs, hoping to find some other type of way back to the first floor so that they eventually find a way out of the building. As they are walking, the smell gets stronger and stronger. The basement smells like something got left outside in the sun, died, and rotted. "If something doesn't change, I think we're going to throw up. This is horrible," cries Brandon.

॥

"Guys, this smells like dead carcass, probably dead rats," says Marie.

Ahead, down the halls, they see a little light shining from the crack of the doors. It's kind of weird because all the power for the building is off.

Brandon suggests, "Perhaps it's in the direction of the power, the school's control panel."

Moving with extreme caution, they approach the suspicious door. Nervous about opening the door, yet desperate to see what's on the other side, they feel they have no choice but to open it. Alex volunteers to open the mysterious door, asking everyone to take a couple of steps back first.

The door makes a loud, squeaky sound as Alex slowly pushes it, cracking it open enough to see what's on the other side. Alex can't see anything, so he pushes the door all the way open. What they see on the other side of the door is entirely unexpected. A horrible, horrible sight! They see Crystal and Martha's bodies hanging in the air with a chain wrapped across their necks, like a meat chop shop. Their bodies are split open down the middle of their chest; all their insides are missing. Puddles of blood build up under their bodies. Next to the two bodies lays an old bloody axe.

Shocked at seeing this dreadful scene, Alex, Brandon, and Marie are disgusted. Their stomachs cringe as they try to hold the vomit in. *This explains why the bodies are disappearing,* thinks Alex. The ghost comes back after he kills someone, storing the bodies in the basement.

"So, this is where the ghost lives or hangs out," whispers Brandon.

Flickering candles burn off the scent of feces. Looking closer, they notice that all the glass candle holders are filled with wax feces. Hands over their nose and mouth, they struggle to explore the room, trying to find a door that will eventually lead them outside. When they see a door, they rush towards it. Pushing with all they have, they try opening it but find it locked tight shut. Brandon walks around trying to find some keys lying around for the door, thinking, *This is the only door in the room that might free us.* All of them begin searching the room.

Marie finds an old rusty cabinet. She starts searching it only to find old school documents. So far, nothing useful. They continue their search. Moving about quickly, there's no telling when the ghost is coming back to this room. A couple of seconds later, heavy footsteps rattle the floor and a dragging sound from what feels like a heavy bag or something similar approaches the locked door. Brandon motions his head, giving his friends the heads up. They try to find a hiding spot quickly. Then they hear the ghost's heavy breathing moving closer to the door.

Now, in silent mode, Marie gets her friends' attention by pointing to a big tablecloth covering an old school table. Everyone crawls to the table, hiding under the tablecloth. *Boom!* They watch the door kicked off its hinges, flying past the table under which the three teenagers hide. The broken wood pieces tumble on the floor. Peeping under the cloth, Alex bites his lips in sadness. Heavy footsteps walk past, dragging James' dead, cold body across the floor, leaving a trail of blood. With their hands over their mouths, Alex, Brandon, and Marie try their best not to make a single sound. The ghost slams James' body across a long metal table. Then he reaches his hand into a large metal maintenance box full of various tools, grabs a hand saw, and steps over to James' body. He slashes his flesh down to the cracking sounds of James' skeleton frame, down to his belly button. Ripping his chest cavity wide open, he grabs all his bloody insides, including stomach, heart, lungs, intestines, liver, gallbladder, urinary bladder, pancreas, spleen, diaphragm, and esophagus. Gutting him like a fish, he grabs a huge heavy black trash bag and throws the parts in the bag.

Alex, Brandon, and Marie are unable to believe their eyes. *Is this really happening?* thought all three of them. Once done cleaning James out, the ghost grabs James' body, throws it over his shoulder, and walks him over to the dead bodies of Alex's missing friends.

Like the others, he wraps a spear chain tightly around his ankles, hanging him upside down. He ties James so tightly that Alex, Brandon, and Marie hear the bones in his ankles crack. The ghost picks up the black garbage bag full of James' guts and walks out of the room. Blood and a thick yellow substance drip from his bag, leaving the door slightly open. The three wait for the heavy footsteps to disappear. As soon as they do, they take their chance. Wanting to see where the other side of the door leads, everyone crawls from under the table and starts tiptoeing to the door.

They slowly crack it open, trying not to let the door squeak. The door leads to another long dark hall with a couple of entries on each side. *Who knows where these doors are going,* wonders Alex.

Slowly walking down the dark halls of the basement, they try each door they pass by. Sadly, they all seem to be locked. Eventually, they come across a door that isn't locked. They enter the darkroom, shinning their flashlights everywhere. It turns out the room is only an old storage space of the school, full of old desks and file cabinets.

Unable to find anything useful, they think it's better not to waste any time. Their search for the way out continues. But just as they are about to leave the little storage room, they hear a loud thud, followed by a *Boom* and a kick to the wall. Alex takes his hand off the doorknob and flashes his light where he thought he heard the noise. He waits for a second, and *bam,* it happens again. There was a closet door in the back of the room. Something was kicking the wall on the opposite side of where they were standing as if someone was inside the closet.

"Brandon, walk with me to the closet. I want to check it," says Alex, mustering up his courage.

Marie holds the flashlight toward the door; just in case something jumps out, they have good lighting. Alex counts one, two, three, and swings open the door. Marie shines the light in the little closet room. Brandon and Alex step back and peek into the closet from a safe distance. Marie gets a closer look and is stunned by what she sees. She is unable to believe her eyes. The flashlight drops from her hand in shock at her visual.

Seeing Marie's shocked face, Alex and Brandon quickly ask her to explain what she saw. Marie is speechless. Then Brandon rushes over and grabs the flashlight. He shines it in the closet and is disbelieved by what he sees.

They witness a horrific, barbaric display of human torture. The last thing they'd expected to stumble upon in the basement was their friend Amelio. Dropping their heads in disbelief, they found it difficult to look at him in this cramped closet, chained up from head to toe. Amelio's legs and hands cuffed and a chain around his wrist tied to a metal water pipe made it impossible for him to move. He's a horrible mess. Still wearing the same clothes from last time, his eyes are tied up. Even his mouth was covered with a blue cloth tied around his head.

Brandon and Marie try and run to him, but Alex grabs them both with a quick reaction, stopping them from going to him. Marie and Brandon pull away, "What's the problem, Alex?" and then, snatching their arms away from him, they continue to say, "It's Amelio! Our friend! Why are you stopping us from helping?"

"What if it's a trap?" whispers Alex.

Silenced by what Alex said, they think of taking another closer look at Amelio. They notice there were old lunch treys by him, surrounded by old moldy food crumbs.

Alex then says, "Stay back and keep the light on him while I check to see if that's really Amelio. If it is Amelio, there's a lot of questions that need to be answered. For one, how he survived this long without starving to death, and, most importantly, why was he kept alive."

Alex approaches Amelio and unties the dirty rags from his eyes and mouth so he can speak. Amelio opens his eyes and couldn't believe what he was seeing. In such disbelief, Amelio scoots back to the wall. He asks them to leave him alone, begging to be released. He thought we were the shadowy ghost figure playing a trick on him. When Amelio starts getting loud, Marie covers his mouth to keep him quiet. They all shushed Amelio and told him that they were not the shadowy ghost figure. "Amelio, we really are who we are. Worry no more, my friend," says Alex.

Amelio just stares at them. He couldn't believe that his friends were down there with him. Just as many questions Alex had for Amelio, Amelio too wished to know everything that Alex had gone through. Soon they begin asking questions.

Alex goes first. He asks Amelio, "How did you survive this long? We were so concerned about you."

Amelio then explains, "The ghost figure comes down into this room daily, at a certain time of the day. He drops off old, leftover food, probably from the school's cafeteria. Then I pick out what looks best to eat. I never knew what he was going to bring to me. It depended on what was for lunch that school day." He goes on to say, "I've had some of the worst things ever. But when you eat to survive, you learn to eat strange things. When you've been starving for days, and that old food sits in front of you for so long, you would eat anything."

"Did that food have any side effects?" asks Marie.

"Oh yes. The stale food has made me sick multiple times. Throwing up and having stomach pains, it feels like you got a stomach full of glass."

The more Amelio told what he's been through, the worse Alex felt for him.

Amelio goes on to say, "The ghost would rarely clean out this area. So, most of the time, the old food that I couldn't eat would attract bugs and mice to this area."

"And he kept you tied up all this time?" asks Brandon.

"Sometimes, the ghost would let me out of my chains. He'd keep the door locked to let me stretch out, but that just happened for a little while. Most of the time, I remained chained up," replies Amelio. Listening to all this blew the minds of Alex and his friends. How he was still alive was a miracle.

Amelio then bursts out in tears, begging Alex to get him out of the chains that had trapped him. "I just want to go home!" Amelio shouted repeatedly.

Without wasting any time, Alex, Brandon, and Marie start to mess with the chains to see how they open. Sadly, they realize that they require some key to release the cuffs as the chains were too thick to break.

Then Amelio says, "The ghost keeps a set of keys with him when he locks me up."

Brandon says, "I remember a bunch of weirdly shaped keys on a desk where the ghost had the bodies hung up at. We all need to go back to find the keys to free Amelio."

Marie speaks up, "Amelio, we will all be right back. We are going to get you free as soon as we find the keys to the chains."

After tying Amelio and covering his eyes and mouth back up, they walk out and close the door, just the way it was. Just in case the ghost comes back and checks on him. They all jog back where they came from—moving quickly with the goal of finding the keys. Once back in the room, they see their dead friends still hanging in the corner. They start to check all the file cabinets and desk draws, searching everywhere from top to bottom. They were only able to find one set of keys. Although these keys didn't look like hand-cuff keys, Brandon keeps them just in case.

Still rambling through the room, Marie comes across an old cabinet. She opens the cabinet doors slightly. In an instance, the door bursts open, and a couple of nasty bats fly out into Marie's face, getting tangled in her hair. Jumping around, swinging at the bats in her hair, Marie begins to panic. Alex and Brandon run up to her to help get the bats out of her hair. Smacking bats left and right, they seem to be coming back to attack Marie. Minutes pass by fighting the bats off, but it seems like they're not going to give up.

Alex's heartbeat is rising as sweat pours off his face. His mouth is dry from swallowing spit and lips dry. He looks around the room to find something to fight the low flying bats off. He spots a fire extinguisher in the corner. Alex sprints to the fire extinguisher and grabs it. He pulls the safety pin off and blasts the bats that are around him to get them off him. Once Alex is free from the bats, he walks up to Marie and Brandon and blasts the bats that are attacking them. Eventually, all the bats fly away into the darkness.

Alex and Brandon are fine, but Marie finds herself bitten a few times by the flying creatures. One on her hand and a couple on her arm and legs. Brandon and Alex try to calm down Marie since she got most of the damage from the bats. Plus, she freaks out about bats and stuff like that anyways.

Alex continues searching for keys while Brandon helps Marie out with her bites. He uses a piece of his shirt to cover the scars and helps put pressure to stop the bleeding. Tying the last piece of the shirt around the last bite, he says, "Marie, once we get out, you need to see a doctor soon. I don't know much about bats or animals, but one thing I can tell is that they carry rabies, which can be dangerous."

Brandon didn't know how long rabies took effect, but he was certain that eventually, it would affect her. As Brandon was explaining that, Alex ran back and whispered to them to hide, "The ghost figure is coming back."

They all rush towards the same place they'd hid the last time, under the table with the white sheet. Just in time!

CHAPTER 12

The Next Escape Strategy

THE GHOST PUSHES THE DOOR WIDE OPEN WITH SUCH force that the entire room jolts. As his muscular feet step inside the room, different tools present on the tables and laboratory bottles up on the shelves begin to rattle. Unaware of why the ghost has returned, Alex and his friends try to remain as quiet as possible. Although freaking out on the inside, they realize the severity of the situation. They keep praying and hoping that none of them gets caught.

I have already lost a lot, I cannot afford to lose any more of my dear friends, thinks Alex as his eyes move from his friends' faces to the ghost's feet. Then almost abruptly, Alex takes a quick peek from under the sheet, watching the ghost move. It feels as though the dark ghost's image is unaware of Alex and his friends' presence. If he'd known, chances were that he would've done something to harm them by now.

Alex, Brandon, and Marie watch the ghost grab more over-sized trash bags. Then he walks to their dead friends hanged brutally in the corner. He takes the bags one by one, and starting from toe to head, he begins to cover the bodies up, tying them with absolute expertise. He repeats the same process with the next bag. Then he takes another trash bag and repeats the process.

Once he is done covering the bodies, he loosens the chains and "thump," the bodies of Alex's dead friends drop to the floor. He picks up all the bodies, throws them over his shoulder, and makes his way to the exit door. *What does he plan on doing with these bodies?* thinks Alex to himself.

On the way out, the ghost accidentally drops his set of keys. He is so engrossed in his mission of getting rid of the corpses that he doesn't even realize dropping his keys. The three boys and girls look at each other, all thinking the same question—*Are these the keys to Amelio's chains?"*

Once Alex and his friends were certain that the ghost has left, they become a bit relieved. Alex, seeing the opportunity, rushes toward the keys on the ground and snatches them up as a starving eagle catches its prey.

Taking a closer look at the set of keys, Alex notices they look a bit weird, almost the shape that matched Amelio's chains. In an instant, Alex stops his inspection of the keys and whispers to his friends, "Hurry up, move quickly before the ghost notices that his keys are missing. But do not make any sound."

The three begin heading back to Amelio with the keys to free him. Much to their relief, they make it back to their friend safely and start unlocking his chains. Amelio tries to stand up. You can tell his body is weak from being down in this dark, cold, drab basement for days. His sense of motivation is strengthening his resolve.

Amelio then says, "Guys, what's your exit plan?"

Alex replies thoughtfully, "Honestly, we're playing it by ear for now. The circumstances kind of dictate our next moves." After a brief pause, he continues, "All that we are certain about right now is that there is a presence of a strange paranormal, ghostly figure in the school, who seems to reign over this building. It is because of his mighty stature that the doors do not open. Even the glass windows are strangely non-breakable."

Brandon speaks up, "We were forced in the basement by the ghost. But now, we need a way out of this hell house by hook or by crook."

After listening to all this, Amelio says, "Maybe I know a way out. An hour after I was captured, I nearly escaped."

Excited about the possibility of their escape, Marie speaks up, "Are you serious, Amelio? How? And where can we break out from?"

"I can't be 100 per cent sure, Marie, but there is a possible way of getting out by going up the stairs to the main halls," answers Amelio.

"That sounds good enough to me," replies Brandon.

"We just need to get out of the basement," Marie whispers, "We need to leave this school completely. No more hiding in classrooms and closets, it is way too risky."

After a while, Amelio speaks up slowly, as if in a trance.

"But... I was recaptured... and chained with more chains," his body shivers lightly as he goes through the scene mentally.

Brandon shakes his head in disappointment. Then an idea pops into his mind, and he shares it with others. "Guys, how about we end this madness by setting the school on fire? The pressure from the heat will cause the windows to explode. Even the doors will loosen. Once the doors are kicked open, then we're free, guys!"

They all look at him like he is crazy.

Then Marie voices her opinion, "I think your idea is pretty stupid. This will get us all killed."

"No, no, chill Marie, I think Brandon has a great idea," jumps in Alex. "Since the ghost is directly connected to the school as he died in this building, this has now become his dwelling place. This is the reason the doors are permanently locked, windows won't break, and all the mess gets cleaned up and damages repaired almost instantly. Trust me when I say he lives here, it's his home."

Brandon, too, supports his friend, saying, "I think Alex is right. Remember the window Martha broke when we first got locked in here just automatically repaired itself."

"Exactly!" Alex continues to say, "And based on some internet searches, I found an article describing a janitor found dead near his janitor's closet from a heart attack. So, it all makes sense now. There is no other way we can think of getting out of here other than smoke and fire."

After thinking for a while, Marie asks, "How are we going to get a big enough fire started to burn this place down?"

Scratching his head, Alex replies, "The only place I can think of is the kitchen. Let the burners send gas fumes out for a couple of minutes, then light it up, making the flames spread throughout. I figure the ghost can't compete with gas, smoke, and fire."

When Alex sees everyone quiet, he asks them, "So, how does the plan sound? Think about it, guys, we've got nothing to lose now. We've already tried our best to leave this place, but have failed each time. This seems to be our only chance now. What do you all think?"

Amelio throws up his hand in favor of the plan. Brandon and Marie agree they must do something drastic.

Then Alex says, "All right, so now we got a plan. Amelio, lead us back to the first floor, out of the basement."

"Down the hall, there should be some stairs that will lead us back to the first floor," says Amelio optimistically.

Within seconds, they ready themselves and start following Amelio to the stairs. Walking down the dark halls, they see a frail, irregular line of blood. *The ghost must have had a leak in one of his trash bags,* thinks Alex. The group then follows the thin trail of blood.

While they're walking through the blood, Amelio is reminded of his friend D'Angelo. He stops midway and directs his attention to Alex, "Dude, dude. Where is D'Angelo? I see it's just two of you guys, and I'm glad you came back to rescue me, but where is D'Angelo? Is my pal all right?" Alex whispers, "I knocked him out, and now he's sleeping in the car outside."

Somewhat amazed and puzzled, Amelio replies, "This is insane, dude. Like wow!" Amelio couldn't believe his ears. The dedication that his friends had shown to rescue him made him feel special and happy.

Alex, Amelio, Brandon, and Marie resume walking.

Walking down the dark halls of the basement, they realize that some of the rooms down there were old and abandoned. Most of these classrooms were cold, dark, creepy, and full of spiders. They all take a couple of peeks in there. Halfway down the hall, Alex tells everyone to hold up. They hear heavy footsteps approaching.

"Hurry," Alex commands. He opens one of the classroom doors for all of them to hide, letting the ghost pass by. They all hid around the corner in an old dusty classroom. The heavy brick-like footsteps pass by.

"Ooohhhh no!" Alex whispers, "We got to go! Right now!"

"What you mean?" asks Amelio, equally scared.

"I think the ghost went back for his keys," Alex tells Amelio.

That's when they all hear a loud sound back from the room where they came from. They realize that once the ghostly apparition sees that Amelio is gone, they're all finished. Alex speaks up nervously, "Amelio, lead the way to the exit. Hurry up!"

Alex, Brandon, Marie, and Amelio rush out of the classroom. *Boom!* a loud explosion rings deep in their eardrums—a shock wave sound behind them. The sound was followed by a crawling flesh, squealing, screaming, almost bringing them to their knee. It was so awfully terrifying that their bodies begin to shake.

The ghost knows Amelio is gone.

Running down the halls, the group stops for a second. They come across three different ways to escape. Amelio looks confused. Marie shrugs her shoulders, pointing to her left. Totally freaking out, Amelio grabs his face. His eyes bucked as more doors bang, shaking the floor beneath them. The ghost is not happy, and he doesn't even try to hide his emotions.

Alex begins to start questioning his future. He's quite confident that at this point, the ghost would break their necks and end his games of terror.

That's when Amelio signals his friends to the right. They keep sprinting down the halls, tripping over books, pens, pencils, broken glass, along with some kind of white gluey substance spread across the halls. Then they see stairs straight ahead of them. They rush towards it excitedly, but in the blink of an eye, the whole scene changes. Behind them, the ghost appears, and everything in its path flies across the halls, crashing and breaking. As they turn to see him, his appearance changes into part-human; a dark creature with a mushroom head, solid neck, and shoulders. His dark body displays skinny arms, clear at the elbow. His long black fingers are visible from a distance. Then he comes near the group, chasing them while grunting like an animal.

I'm pretty sure he's going to break our necks, thinks Alex. Their pace quickens as they successfully reach the staircase.

Once at the stairs, they bent over, completely out of breath. While trying to get it together, they spring up the stairs. The ghost feels only at an arm's distance away. They can feel his hot vomit-smelling breath on their backs, grossly streaming in their nostrils.

One more set of steps to go up, and Alex can see the door to the first floor. He slams through the door, holding it open for the others to run through. Brandon and then Marie run through. Amelio is the last one to enter.

Alex slams the door shut on the ghost, and they take off, running to the nearest classroom. Behind them, *Boom!* as the door they'd just closed explodes.

Marie spots a nearby library, pointing everyone in its direction. They head to the back, hiding behind some bookshelves. A couple of seconds later, the ghost breaks the library door open. Between his odor, his scary monstrous-looking body, all this at one unexpected time is enough to give them a heart attack.

The ghost just stands there, looking around as if no one was in the room.

Alex's heart rate speeds up. At this point, they're all breathing heavily, quietly, and quickly catching their breaths. It is hard to carry out this simple, natural process of breathing when you have basically run for miles to save your lives. Especially Amelio, he's kind of heavy—almost 300 pounds and 6' tall. This dude loves fast foods.

Trying their best to stay quiet, the ghost starts walking around, knocking nearby bookshelves to the floor. At this point, everyone is in the back of the library, except for this creature, who is in the front. Books fly off the shelves, and chairs move from one side of the room to the next. This guy is not happy. As this ghostly creature walks towards Alex and his friends, they all walk to the side of the library, slowly creeping toward the exit door. The ghost's emotions are becoming more erratic, banging his body against the wall screaming, "Now!" It feels like he is destroying the library.

A couple of flying books smack Brandon across the head a couple of times. It looks like an active tornado inside the library. Making matters worse, the ghost starts walking around, flipping *everything* in sight. Amelio escaping from his little prison cell really made the ghost upset. The further the ghost got in the back of the library, the closer the teenagers got to the front. They all take a second to look back at the hidden, shadowy ghost figure. Making sure he can't hear or spot them, all of them tiptoe out of the library.

Going down the hall, walking like they are walking on thin ice, they get as far away from the library as possible. Heading to the end of the hallway and going around the corner, Amelio needs to take a breather. He lays his back against the lockers to take a break and regain his strength. Then Alex whispers, "Our next move to light this place on fire has to be solid. Starting a kitchen fire sounds like a great idea, but I feel like we need something else to really get the fire started."

"What do you mean? What's on your mind, Alex?" asks Marie, bewildered.

"I'm thinking of a good fire starter, something that's not easy to put out. The science room is full of chemicals they use for projects, and the janitor's closet has several chemicals too. If we combine them, emptying all the bottles on the floor, and cut all the gas stoves on, we might get what we're hoping for. If we just let the gas fumes build up, and light the area up, we would surely get our job done. Hopefully, the ghost can't stop that."

While Alex is still talking, weird things start happening around them. The hallway lights rapidly begin flicking off and on. Amelio feels something wet and cold running down his back. He turns around and sees blood oozing down the locker walls. All of them back up into each other in the middle of the halls as they watch the blood pour from the lockers, dripping to the floor. Alex directs everyone toward the janitor's closet to grab supplies and chemicals for the fire. Speed walking down the halls and lights going crazy, all the walls are now sweating blood. Not aware of what is to come next, they get closer to the janitor's closet.

That's when the lights shut off, back to the darkness.

Brandon grabs his little flashlight and shines it down the hall. In the distance, they all see a human shadow run pass by. "Oh shit!" says Brandon and ends up dropping his flashlight on the floor. The only ray of light that Brandon had shuts off with its fall. Brandon, on all fours crawling on the floor, searches for the flashlight. "I can't find it," he whispers, "It's too dark." Now everyone is on the floor, using their hands to feel for his flashlight.

Marie finds the flashlight and tries to cut it on, but no luck. A couple of seconds later, Brandon whispers, "I found it." He turns on the light and shines it on Marie. Marie looks down and notices that what she holds in her hand is not a flashlight but something else, something absolutely awful.

Marie screams and throws the object across the hall, hitting the wall and fast to the floor. Turns out it was a bloody body part from a cut-up wrist and hand. Light shining on the decapitated hand, Brandon says, "Oh my god, look!"

The hand and wrist slowly crawl toward Marie. It jumps in the air towards her, and Brandon runs up to it while Marie screams in her hand, trembling uncontrollably. Brandon knocks the hand away across the hall with his flashlight. That's when the hand crawls away into a classroom, disappearing in the dark. "It's creepy. We need to get going," mutters Brandon.

They head around the corner, up the hall, spotting a large janitor closet. Running up to it, they realize they still have the keys they stole from the ghost. They used them to open the closet door. Looking all around, Alex grabs huge trash bags and starts taking all the chemicals in sight. He stuffs the bag full of all-purpose cleaner, Windex, bowl cleaner and all types. It didn't matter what kind; they were all flammable. Alex fills up the bag. Seeing him, Amelio grabs a bag, too, and repeats what Alex did. Filling the bags up as much as he can, he ties up the bag and passes it to Alex. Brandon, too, grabs a bag and starts filling it up.

Then the craziest thing happens—a long, dark ghostly, skinny arm morphs out of a locker, reaching after Marie.

Marie freezes in place. Amelio runs, tackling her away from the creature's black hand, but he misses. The ghost keeps chasing. As Brandon exits the closet, a dark half-black, half-white arm with long black fingers grabs Brandon by the neck and picks him up. Then the hand throws him back into the closet. Brandon, nearly 6'4" with a football-player frame, lands in a large metal mop bucket and gets stuck. The ghost turns his head, and everyone sees his eyes all red. Black fumes ooze from the pores of his body. Watching in horror, they're all in shock. He walks with force, swinging his arms side to side toward Brandon.

Wheels squeaking, Brandon tries his best to get out of the mop bucket but can't. He struggles to twist and turn, trying to wiggle his large frame but is wedged. When he landed in the mop bucket, he tried to use his hand to break his fall, but that didn't work. In fact, he ended up springing his wrist. Not being able to get out, the ghost walks into the closet and shuts the door behind him. Before anyone can attempt to save Brandon, he screams with fear in his voice, saying, "Run, guys! Just get the job done without me. I'll fight this thing so you can get the hell out!"

Emotionally, it's tough to leave their friend behind, but they need to act, and they need to act fast. So, they decide to move ahead. Alex signals the rest to start running. Marie and Amelio disagree, saying they want to stay and help Brandon.

"It's too late," Alex shouts. Then grabbing his bag full of chemicals, he tells them to grab the other bags. "Let's go to the science room. NOW!"

They grab the other bags and take off to the next location in a rush.

The face of a monstrous ghost, blood-shot red eyes, smiles, as he stands over Brandon, laughing and staring at him, struggling to get out of the mop bucket. The ghostly figure looks side to side. Then he takes his skinny jet-black long fingers, and grabs a bottle of lime away—an acid-type chemical used to clean hard water spots off sinks. This is such a powerful chemical that it has the tendency to burn flesh through clothes. If it gets under the skin, it will burn it, causing horrible itching and burning pains. Gushing sounds of slow-dropping thick liquid pouring down Brandon's head can be heard clearly. The ghost has begun opening, emptying the entire industrial cleaning bottles onto Brandon's body. Then the ghostly creature grabs more bottles, repeating the same process. He smiles at Bandon, and then laughing hysterically, empties three bottles on Brandon's face and body.

"Somebody help me please, aah, oh my god!" screams Brandon as the chemicals burn his skin and begin boiling up. Chemical in his eyes, and mouth, burns everything it touches. The ghost is enjoying the sight, watching him squirm in excruciating pain and screaming at the top of his lungs. He sees Brandon's legs kicking in the air, jerking from the pain, then kicking as the acid burns, causing him to defecate, overflowing his mop bucket with liquid diarrhea.

Now the ghost looks around the room for more chemicals to use. The ghost finds one more bottle of lime away and cracks it open. He goes to Brandon and picks up his burning body while he writhes in pain. The ghost makes Brandon open his mouth, but Brandon wouldn't let him. Frustrated to see his disobedience, the dark ghostly figure squeezes his large fingers tighter around Brandon's jaw, slowly cracking his jaw wide open. Then using his other hand, he begins pouring chemicals from a bottle of Lime Away down his throat.

Forcing the hot green acid down his throat, Brandon slams his muscular frame to the floor. The ghost enjoys watching Brandon gag, reaching his long arms in the air for help, choking, and spitting up blood. He likes seeing him bubbling on the ground from the acid, burning his insides, and foaming from the mouth.

The last thing Brandon sees is the ghost standing over him, watching him suffer. Shaking out of control, Brandon's eyes pop out of its sockets, and he dies on the floor as his body boils on the inside.

Brandon's lifeless body remains on the floor with blood and acid pouring out of his mouth. The ghostly figure grabs the wet body and throws Brandon over his shoulder. Then he takes him away back to the basement and cuts him up like a fish.

Alex and his friends look out the window and see the dark ghostly figure take a large trash bag to the dumpster, as he did to the other bodies. He leaves a smaller clear on the side as they watch.

CHAPTER 13

Deviant Friend

RED PAW PAD PRINTS PRESSED AGAINST A MUDDY ground can be seen moving toward a shallow grave slowly. Chester drags a large, clear bloody trash bag containing a human heart, lungs, urinary bladder, liver, pancreas spleen, kidneys, along with the small and large intestines. Then suddenly, the sound of the plastic bag being dragged along the moist ground stops. Gentle fog rolls across the shallow graves as Chester's bloodied paws digs a deeper hole. A beating heart pulsating inside the clear garbage bag can be heard in the dead of night.

The digging stops.

Long brown hairy dog legs move toward the trash bag and stop abruptly. A muddy, bloody paw repeatedly stomps on the moving human heart inside the bag, but the heart refuses to surrender. It keeps pulsating. Puzzled, the dog puts his nose near the heart and sniffs. Then he licks the outside of the plastic. Before he knows it, his white teeth chew a hole on the surface of the trash bag. Then with the help of his long black claws and muddy paws, Chester makes the hole larger.

As soon as the heart is visible, the dog sniffs and then licks it. Chester touches its movement with his paw. One more lick, and Chester lays his body next to the bag, sinking his teeth in the dying heart. He now holds it between his canines. Enticed by its waft, saliva begins to drool from his fangs, falling on the plastic bag present below. The heart stops moving as Chester chews on it. After swallowing it hurriedly, he smacks his lips and walks back to the grave to continue digging.

After nearly twenty minutes of digging, sharp canines grab the plastic bag containing human guts and pull it into a four-foot-deep grave. His short tail facing the grave begins to cover the trash bag—now inside the grave—with undug soil. Rapidly pushing the soil between his legs, he tries his best to hide the human remains.

After working tirelessly for two hours, he succeeds in covering up the sadistic mutilations carried out by Palmyra High School's ghost.

Slowly walking between several trees, the ghostly figure watches the Doberman drag body parts deep into the woods. A malicious grin spreads across his countenance as he heads back inside his dwelling.

* * *

A mouse slips across the bloodied concrete basement floor inside Palmyra High School's maintenance room. A metal table present in the corner is littered with the internal human organs of the ghost's victims. Present near the table, the ghost is seen busy carving the organs with expertise, one at a time. A half-clear, half-dark hand with spaghetti string flesh hanging from the arm scrapes the bloody human guts out and puts them inside another clear trash bag.

Under a full moon outside the school's back door sits the red Doberman near four commercial trash bins. From the reflection of the moon, he looks like an ethereal figure, almost like a bronze statue at attention. With his tall ears pointed toward the sky, large paws firmly planted in the ground, and long nose pointed in the direction of the back door, he remains still, waiting patiently. His olive-shaped eyes glowing red tell a tale unknown—the tale of being possessed by the entity that resides within the school.

Who would've thought that this highly trained, award-winning Doberman would one day be under the demonic spell of an evil master? This second master exploited the dog's intelligence for his own selfish means and trained him to advance the recording of his own lost soul's pain and suffering.

It all began when Chester first noticed Biff's diary and held it between his fangs to give it to the professor. The moment Chester's saliva touched the surface of the black composition book, a demonic force was triggered. It entered Chester's body quickly, tapping into the DNA of the breed. Immediately the ghost's spirit channeled the dog. It wasn't difficult for the ghost to find out what Chester's breed was. Doberman Pinschers are a fearless, intelligent, and vigilant breed. This breed loves to please as they have an excellent temperament. The ghost was able to sense the Doberman's kind as good-natured, protective, and affectionate, and decided to take advantage of his qualities. He knew very well that the dog would protect him and remain a loyal companion, something he didn't wish to lose.

Shortly after discovering Biff's diary, Chester began shaking and whining while sleeping one night. His restlessness woke him up, and he sat, looking up towards the sky attentively and then down, around him. That was the first time he began listening to secret voices and sounds that humans could not hear. It was only later that he found who the speaker was. It was the ghostly spirit of Biff, Chester's new master.

Soon, Chester begins serving two masters.

* * *

Heavy raindrops fall, occasionally tapping on another bloody trash bag that Chester pulls near a freshly dug shallow grave. His long brown nose and white teeth tug on it as raindrops roll off Chester's back. But no amount of rain affects the Doberman. He stays adamantly near the grave and does his job responsibly.

When Chester looks at the trash bag closely, something catches his attention. In an instance, his ears tilt to the side and his tongue hangs out. As he continues to look at the bag fixedly, he begins to pant, breathing heavily out of exhaustion. Then the long brown snout sniffs the garbage bag and notices another pulsating heart. He bites through the plastic, eating the heart, lungs, and urinary bladder. Instead of burying the whole plastic bag, he pushes off the remaining human guts into the grave, dropping them in one by one. Then using his nose, he covers the grave.

By this time, the rainfall stops, and the pale moon becomes visible high up in the sky. Low fog rolls over the tops of four grave mounds, enveloping them in an eerie atmosphere. Chester sits near the mounds, gazing at them as if intending to protect his work. The ghost watches his loyal animal and is satisfied with the sight. Then nodding his head, he walks away, disappearing into the deep woods.

After digging and then guarding the shallow graves the entire night, Chester starts getting exhausted but makes sure not to show any signs of tiredness. Then an hour before sunrise, he walks back to the school. Faithful to his ghostly master, Chester sits outside the high school. There, he waits attentively for his second master to finish recording his nightly episodes about the trapped teenagers inside Palmyra High School. Just as the sun's upper limb appears to cross the horizon, the ghost walks through the high school's back door onto a misty football field and hands Chester his diary as he did every morning.

The ghost then looks at Chester and, pointing his glowing finger at the dog's forehead, uses telepathy to communicate. Through telepathy, he tells the Doberman when and where to place the diary, reminding him to bring it back in time so that he keeps recording his activities. Chester responds by standing up on two legs and staring into the ghost's profound eyes, barking and howling.

Coming home after working hours for his second master, Chester uses his sturdy canines to turn on an outside water spigot.

He closes his eyes as water removes blood and mud off his large body. Shaking his body rapidly, he attempts to dry his entire coat. Once satisfied with his appearance, he sneaks into the house, finishing his drying off in front of the living room fireplace. Then taking a deep breath, he curls up in a ball, falling into a deep slumber.

The first master's Doberman enjoys chasing scores of whitetail rabbits throughout his owner's estate. Occasionally, Chester chases foxes off the property using his quick horizontal movements back and forth. Then standing on his two hind legs, he freaks them out. He walks toward them rapidly, barking and growling them away.

Hallways of the States, a popular children's hospital in Nebraska, reflects the red Doberman's happy face, gracing its hospital with head up high and ears pointed straight.

"Hi, Chester, good seeing you again," waves a doctor walking in the opposite direction. Greeted with waves and even a few quick hugs by nurses and doctors throughout the hospital, Chester makes his way to the room of an eight-year-old cancer patient. He slowly walks toward little Peter's hospital bed and looks at the bald boy intently. Peter's big blue eyes light up, and a huge smile spreads on his face as he stretches his arms toward Chester. Chester directs his long brown face in Peter's welcoming hands. Peter places his face on top of the dog's warm brown and gold head. Tears stream down the parents' eyes who stand on the opposite side of Peter's bed. The kid's mom blows her nose just as Chester climbs onto Peter's bed, allowing Chester to hug and stroke his shiny brown short hair coat.

"Hi, Chester, I love you. Chester, will you be my friend?" asks Peter innocently. Chester answers with a lick on his cheek. Parents take pictures as they hug and stroke the Doberman. Soon afterward, the doctor comes into the room. He pets Chester as nurses prepare to take the eight-year-old for another surgery. "Chester, I hope I can see you again after my surgery. I love you, my friend," says Peter.

Peter strokes Chester as he hops off the bed and sits at attention, watching Peter being rolled out of his room for his cancer procedure. His parents hug Chester. Then the two adults walk behind their son, who's being wheeled out of the room.

* * *

Early morning, striking sunrays touch the breeze against the new cherry blossoms. Nature calls throughout the treetops and to Chester's bladder. Opening the back-den door and running far from the professor's mansion, Chester lifts his leg in front of a maple tree, finally relieving his loaded nighttime bladder. Chester has the day off from his hospital compassion visits and can spend some routine dog time that includes running around chasing rabbits.

As dawn approaches, Chester stops in his track toward home. Raising his 110-pound muscular frame in the air, he only stands on his two hind legs. He spins his head from side to side, ears moving like an antenna as if trying to listen to a high-frequency voice that only he can detect. A bloody, lifeless, mangled skin of a body squeaks against a shiny waxed hallway. Holding its hand is the ghost's dark glowing hand, pulling it to the school's maintenance room. "Come, come, Chester. I need you, buddy. We have unfinished work waiting for you at the school. Stop everything and come now!" commands the ghost.

But then, at the estate, a familiar voice calls, "Chester, Chester, come here. It's time to eat breakfast. Where are you? Come, boy!" calls the professor. Moving his head back and forth, from side to side in the direction of master one and two, the dog seems to be confused. The large Doberman sits at attention, torn between two masters, thinking which one to respond to. Rolling on his back with his front and back legs in the air, he continues to move from one side to another. Then he suddenly stops, and his ears droop down.

The ghost morphs his own body through the high school roof, letting out a loud, disturbing sound capable of shaking people with fear. Chester notices the sound but decides to ignore it at first. He's preoccupied with animal play, chasing rabbits, and running away from the fox. Running back and forth, when the horizon approaches Chester, he takes off like lighting, running at a fast pace. All the muscles in his body display his might, his focused call to duty for his second master hours later. Soon, a sleek, sturdy Doberman's silhouette races in front of windy moon-lit dawn toward the high school. Stars can be seen twinkling under a full moon, and beneath, the sounds of Chester's feet galloping on the ground can be heard from a distance. His nostrils are sounding off to the rhythm of each large paw striking the ground as he gets closer to the back entrance of Palmyra High School.

Satisfied with his internal vision of Chester running toward the school, the ghost morphs back inside. Picking up one of his dead victims' hands, he takes it with the intent to gut it. After some time, a clear bloody trash bag is tossed outside the school's maintenance door at the back. Slowly walking toward the gutted carved-out human insides, Chester pulls the hefty trash bag towards his usual grave-side route. Through several wood trees and mud, Chester passes raccoons, skunks, rabbits, and foxes that mysteriously watch a member of the animal kingdom drag what most of them would consider a good meal for the evening and devour within minutes. The aura coming from Chester's body freezes their natural instincts and desires, stopping them in their tracks. They become somewhat like statues, unable to move their body. Only their eyes move now and then, watching the Doberman's actions closely. Sniffing with their noses the air that lurks around, they find themselves unable to react to the tempting human remains inside the plastic trash bag. The sound of crickets echoes in the background of the site, where three mounds protrude out of the burial grounds created by Chester. With dense trees nearby, this area seems to be hidden away secretly.

Large paws furiously dig, making a deeper hole to place into the earth yet another bloodied plastic garbage bag containing human guts. After digging for three long hours nonstop, Chester pulls out large rocks with his teeth from the surrounding area. Then he removes tree roots, cans, and other materials in the way. Chester collapses in the middle of his freshly-dug grave, licking his aching and wet paws. Above his head swirls a gigantic bat that whisks past his head, nearly touching his tall ears.

Jumping to his feet and then on two hind legs, Chester hops around in an attempt to catch the bat. He even jumps three feet high in the air, but all in vain. Frustrated for being unable to kill his nighttime irritation, Chester begins to bark. His growling produces foam at the tip of his mouth. Then all of a sudden, taking a running start like an Olympic pole vaulter, Chester hurls his muscular, sleek frame near the bat—now some six feet in the air—and succeeds in snapping the flying creature. He then grabs a small portion of the black bat's long wing. Both fall to the ground some five feet apart.

Chester rolls over on all fours breathing heavily, walking slowly with caution in his eyes, tongue hanging and dripping toward the noticeably fallen wounded bat. Leaping toward the bat in midair, Chester slowly lays down, placing his large paws over the bat. The bat squirms underneath Chester's legs and pushes its entire body with such force that the Doberman loses control. The large bat lands on top of Chester's back, biting the side of his long neck.

Yelp! Yelp! Yelp! The cries of Chester echo far and wide. Chester's body rolls to the side. He licks the side of his neck with his long pink tongue several times.

That's when the bat turns into a cloud of black streaming smoke, revealing its original identity. Within seconds, the bat turns into the ghost of Palmyra High School. Standing nearly 6'4" tall, displaying his full-size dark head monstrous, the gray matter replaces human skin. The Doberman is surprised to see the ghost's black mouth, nose, large holes instead of eyes, and a tumor-like hump protruding from his cervical spine at the back of his head. The upper portion of his gray ghostly body show black lines running along the surface. His skinny arms and bones glow white with spaghetti strings of flesh hanging from the sides of his body.

The Doberman remains on the ground with his ears pent down to the side of his head. The short, snub tail points down as the ghost levitates in the air, with glowing eyes beaming red. The ghost then points his middle finger in the direction of Chester. Now looking up directly into the ghost's eyes, what Chester experiences next shakes him from within. The ghost sends a single lightning bolt to the dog's eyes that collapses Chester. Then dissolving into the night sky, the ghost disappears.

* * *

Wobbly legs trying to get balance like a newborn colt, Chester tries several times to regain balance. After several attempts, the Doberman continues with his duties of placing the plastic bag into the shallow dug grave. Noticing another beating heart, Chester opens the bag and eats all the contents present inside. Moments later, he lets out a loud gulp, sending hundreds of small chunks of human guts all over the shallow grave. Chester growls at the grave and does his job of covering the grave heartlessly this time. As he runs away, back to his first master's home, nature's wild animals converge on the human guts left behind by Chester at the shallow gravesite.

Another black bat follows Chester, this time stopping in front of his face and forcing Chester to stop in his tracks. Their pupils connect. Although no words are spoken and no action takes place, Chester knows what he is to do. He turns around and starts moving back in the direction of Palmyra High School with the large bat leading the way and dissolving in a puff of black smoke into the night air again.

Chester sits attentively on the high school 50-yard football field, waiting like a loyal soldier for the latest diary recording of the ghostly encounter in the school. When the ghost appears with the diary in his hand, Chester wags his short tail and lays down his body in submission. He looks at the ghost with respect while his ears signal fear. Small drops of blood on the outer surface of his diary are visible.

Chester's canine teeth gently clamp down on the book. Then he stands on his two hind legs as if to show respect to his second master. Coming down on all fours, he soon takes off in the direction of Ariel's house, running like a wild steed.

CHAPTER 14

Encountering the Chief

CHESTER SPRINTS HIS ONE-AND-A-HALF FOOT 80-POUND frame through a wooded area dashing toward Palmyra High School for nearly two miles without stopping. After arriving at the destination, he sits outside the school and looks at the partially lit basement and top floor of the building. For the next two hours, winds continue to swirl, and lightning flashes the sky like a fourth of July celebration. But despite the weather, Chester sits at attention like an army soldier on guard duty.

The Doberman runs up to the dumpster and continues to sit in attention. With his dark, somber eyes, he watches the ghostly figure dump one bag into the dumpster, leaving a second clear trash bag full of what looks like red and gray slimy substance. From the highly intelligent Doberman's visual perspective, he sees human lungs, liver, heart, intestines, gallbladder, and human guts. The ghostly apparition then retreats, leaving the human corpse for the dumpster. Like an honest, dedicated worker, the Doberman picks up the bag and begins his task at once.

Watching the dog from one of the school's windows, Alex is intrigued by the Doberman's presence and precise movements. He is somewhat impressed by the dog's skills of secretly and strategically stacking the bags behind a second dumpster. After running some two miles throughout the foggy, murky woods filled with the sound of large frogs and neck biting mosquitoes, the Doberman often falls in the woody, almost swamp and soppy forest, only to get up again.

With the passion for finding out what the hell this Doberman is up to, Alex stops and observes the dog using the binoculars bought earlier during their equipment purchase. He sees the dog digging faster and faster. After making a crater more than seven feet deep, the dog drags the bag into the hole. As soon as that is done, he buries the bag hurriedly. The red athletic Doberman finishes his task only to dash off back in the direction of Palmyra High School. Frustrated with the total madness, Alex walks closer to the window and notices numerous dirt mounds around the same area. From the human remains scattered near the mounds, Alex concludes that this Doberman is burying the guts of those people who were once his friends. This realization makes Alex sick to his stomach and he throws up several times. He tries to break the window while his heart weeps, thinking about the friends he'd lost and the havoc that was brought upon him and his team. Unable to break the window, Alex begins to sob hopelessly. As his concerned friends come near him, he watches the Doberman run out of the wooded area into a dark, pitch-black vicinity.

* * *

While the Doberman is gone, the dark ghostly figure sits down in a classroom. As per routine, he takes his blood-soaked index finger and writes about his latest encounter ending in death in his black composition diary. Thirty minutes later, the Doberman comes back and is handed the book outside the building by the ghostly figure. The Doberman heads home, leaping the estate's eight-foot fence, and places the book at the front door. Chester tries to clean himself by rolling in the grass and running through the ground's water sprinkler system, trying to clean his body and getting rid of the human blood.

* * *

My doorbell rings quickly twice, as if by someone in a rush. Before getting up and opening the door, I take out my cell phone, thinking of looking through the surveillance camera to find out who the visitor is. As soon as I turn the application on, I see no one—there is nothing but silence. I move over the mechanical camera and notice a bloody black book. "Not this again," I murmur. I walk to the front door to make sure what I saw a few seconds back was actually there and not a fragment of my imagination.

There it was, the book that possessed the power of mysteriously getting back to me somehow. But instead of ignoring the deadly diary, a voice within me forces me to read it. I get a mask and gloves, pick up the book from one corner, and once again take it to my garage. Standing, as usual, I read the latest encounter that is, like the previous incidents, equally disturbing and horrifyingly brutal. With each page that I turn over, my heart beats faster.

Going through the book this time, I learn the ghost victims' bodies are slit open like gutted fish. As for the remains, it's never explained in the writings. Reading the crap always makes me sick to my stomach, leading me to have nightmares, drinking, and smoking more pipe tobacco and cigars. This is grotesque and sick shit, not fit for an average human to read and digest. Yet I knew this crap had appeared in real time. Often, I felt as though something, or perhaps someone, was watching me—an invisible force watching my every move. Thinking about these thoughts makes me scared about myself and my precious dog. "What's going on?" I look here and there as if waiting for some response.

The next day, as soon as the sun comes out and I'm back from my usual jogging routine, I decide to continue my online research to satisfy my curiosity about the book and dead bodies. Within a few minutes, the weather begins to change. Heavy rains start beating down on my house roof-top, and heavy winds soon pick up. Chester jumps up, insisting he has to get outside. Once he's outside and taking a dump near the property fence, there is a wimping sound. I look for signs of him and call his name but am met with silence. No response? Where did he go?

Grabbing my raincoat and umbrella, I walk outside and continue to call Chester. Trying not to panic, I grab my keys, get in my truck with high beams on, looking for my most faithful and trusted friend. Small tree branches fall in front of my drive, my windshield wipers on full speed, pounding rains cause me to drive only five miles per hour. Now a gravel road but still no sign of Chester. Winds pick up, and on the radio, the weather service alerts for hail and tornado. I turn around, barely able to see. The winds are so strong that my truck is moving as if on its own. Just as I start pulling over, lightning strikes a tree in front of me. I open my door and roll out in the nick of time as it crushes the truck. I manage to walk about a half a mile in the hail and heavy rains. When I get inside my estate, now almost evening, I go toward the book, but to my surprise, it's gone! And just like that, it stops raining. Dark black clouds begin clearing as I look outside; the sky is now filled with stars. Still no Chester. Exhausted, I try to stop worrying about the Doberman. "I believe he will arrive home by sunrise."

* * *

A soaking wet Chester runs at a racehorse pace towards Ariel's house with a blood-dripping composition diary of the ghost of her husband between his white canine teeth. At night, Ariel walks past the old master room. The stench from his rotten spirit floats throughout the room that instantly catches her attention. Ariel stands afar, unaware of Biff's ghostly presence. Taking in the odor and the many memories of her husband, she places his bloodied diary on their old desk.

Moments later, Ariel witnesses Chester, the Doberman, bring the diary into their room. Tiptoeing in her bare feet, she quietly goes to the broom closet, reaching for her shotgun. As soon as she pulls it toward her eye to aim at the dog, he stares down the double-barrel shotgun and, sensing the danger, darts through the window. *BAM BOOM,* a missed shot toward Chester not successful. At the stroke of midnight, Ariel is startled awake to a loud banging sound. Walking in the sound's direction, Ariel notices that the banging gets louder. At first, she hesitates and slows down her pace before walking into her old master bedroom. A dark ghostly image casts his image over the desk. A 6'3" frame image standing alone, the ghostly image is seen pounding the desk.

Ariel runs inside the room, grabs the book, and with tears streaming down her eyes, says, "Bif,f honey, you can't keep doing this. It's time to rest in peace. If you don't stop soon, you're never going to crossover your stay in purgatory. I want to meet you in Heaven, babe."

Biff's ghostly shadowy figure turns over the office desk and walks in the direction of the bedroom wall, walking through into the street and then disappearing into the sky.

There were numerous but failed attempts to communicate with her dead husband when she appeared in the room. She remembers leaving coffee on the desk only to find the cup empty the next morning. Ariel hears a nose in her former master room. She calmly goes into the kitchen, makes two cups of coffee, pouring a small amount of milk in one cup marked hers and dark coffee with sugar into a second coffee mug marked his. She walks inside their former master bedroom and places the oversized red mug on their old charred desk. On the desk sits the black composition book. It opens to a blank white page. While Ariel is still trying to figure out what all this means, a dark shadowy figure appears, and a hand begins writing in red ink,

"You ain't seen nothing yet!"

The book closes.

* * *

Strange 24 hours...

Since research is in my doctorial DNA, I read everything that came my way regarding the high school and its janitors, particularly Biff. During my research, I came across two detailed and useful articles. One of them was an obituary of Biff, the janitor. Through the obituary, I learned that Biff's wife is the same woman I interacted with at the Chronicle, named Ariel. She is an heir to the newspaper and owns 50 per cent of the town's real estate. The second article detailed how Biff had died of a heart attack. It also talked about his military background and a history of heart complications. As I kept reading, I noticed how much the Palmyra High School students respected and appreciated him and his wife. Also, how Biff believed in honoring students for their academic performance.

Is it possible that the spirit of the dead janitor is killing the folks who enter the high school after sundown, as narrated in the black composition book? I begin wondering. *Does my Doberman have to do anything with the book or its owner? I hope not.*

I keep looking for other articles but realize there are none about the killings in the local paper owned by Biff's wife. Intrigued, I drive over to the nearest town and find articles about a missing person found in a dumpster with no insides and completely gutted, somewhat like a fish. The articles were never published on the internet and were only sent to Associated Press, just stored on flash drives.

Since Biff's ghost, the janitor, never wrote in his diary about where he put the dead bodies, I decided to figure it out on my own. Without any further delay, I went to the local police station with one chief of police and the mayor of the village. When I met his assistant deputy, he says, "You cannot meet the chief right away. You must make an appointment to see him."

"Make an appointment first? But that's crazy. I can damn near spit across the street and be in the next town." My frustration was evident through my tone. That's when I begin to think that something smells weird. But since it isn't wise to mess with the police officials, I decide to leave.

Just as I'm walking toward my pickup truck that had to be repaired after being struck by lightning earlier, I see this black police SUV pull up. The car had a black German Shepard baking his ass off in the Palmyra police station's direction. I walk toward a short 5'6" guy and, mustering up my courage, ask as politely as possible, "Sir, are you the police chief?"

"Yeah. Who the hell wants to know?" he retorted.

I see the police chief badge on his chest and, in a respectful tone, I reply, "I'm Professor Kneel, sir." Before I could get a word out next, he interrupts, "What are you looking for, some research about my town or something?" says the police chief.

The dog in the back of his SUV keeps barking his ass off, making it difficult for me to state why I was there. The chief just stands there looking at me with these dark aviator sunglasses on. I finally blurt out, "I'm researching the story behind missing persons and everything regarding them. For instance, where were they last seen, or who they interacted with? My question is, are they still investigating possible deaths or murders at the high school over the past year or so?"

The chief sucks his teeth, takes the toothpick in his mouth, sticks it near the rear of this teeth, and pulls out a large piece of red meat, "Sir, you sticking your nose in my business. This is my town and my investigation. It's best you get back to the university, and leave police business up to me," he replies in a stern, threatening manner. He tips his hat and hollers to his dog, "Shut the fuck up!" Then he turns his body away from me and walks into the police station. I stand there in amazement as the office door closes.

For the next two weeks, I keep reading this twisted diary from time to time, describing various acts of gruesome murders. One day, I find Chester near this book, sniffing and trying to open it up. Watching from one corner, I see the Doberman panting heavily, moving near the book restlessly. Something about his odd behavior makes me feel as if my dog has a connection with this book. At that moment, I recall how the editor of the local town's newspaper, the widower of the freaking ghost, gave me a cold stare when I asked for information regarding the janitor and the high school.

When my head begins spinning with 'what-ifs' and 'maybes,' I decide to take a break. That evening, I think of visiting the local tavern and have a few drinks.

At the bar, I see the chief's assistant deputy, "Give this good man two shots of your finest whisky. On me!" says the deputy to the bartender loudly. Then he looks at me and says, "I hear you met the Chief without that appointment I told you needed. Honestly, the chief doesn't like too much being questioned about his job. And well, that understandable; he's been running this town for 20 years."

I down the two shots and speak up, "Thank you for the drinks. I just wanted to know about the missing bodies." The moment I say this, the tavern goes quiet. The music stops playing, so do the guys at the pool table, and a weird hush comes over the room. Some 30 eyes are glued on me, and I just don't know how loud I was.

At the far end of the bar, a tall, gorgeous woman with long dark hair and red fingernails, wearing a short leather dress, looks at me with cold purple eyes. Her red lips and ashen skin looked like she had been embalmed. With her eyes fixed on me, she speaks up from the far end of the bar, "Honey, if I were you, I'd stop asking about bodies around here. You're retired from that fancy university up the road. You might want to just take it easy and keep an eye on that dog of yours."

The moment she stops speaking, the music goes back to playing. Even the guys shoot pool, and the bar chatter continues. Bewildered, I look at the bartender, who slides me two more shots. I drink them and look back in the direction of the gorgeous woman. To my surprise, she is gone. I look around, but she is nowhere to be seen. I walk to the bathroom area and then back towards the bar, but nothing. I ask the bartender, "Where did she go? Did you see her leave?"

"Who are you talking about?"

"That tall woman, wearing a short leather dress. The one who was right there at the end of the bar. Where did she go?"

"I think you've had too much to drink tonight. I didn't see no woman, mister."

I had come to the pub with the intention of calming my nerves, but the reverse had happened. Exhausted, I get inside my car and start driving home. Two minutes from my estate's gate, I see blue and red blinking lights reflect on my rearview mirror and the glass of my car. I hear, "Pull over now, sir, pull over." I do as instructed.

Soon, the chief walks over. The moment I roll down my window, I explain to the chief, "Sir, I am just two minutes away from home."

Ignoring my pleas, the chief asks, "Have you been drinking?"

"Yes, I have but—"

He goes to his car and then comes back again. He administers a breath test, then says, "I want you to step out and take a sobriety test."

To my relief, I pass the test. But then he says, "I'm taking you into the station for suspicion of DUI."

"What? No, please, sir. I beg you, please, let me go home. I'll walk home if you want."

"Get in the back of my squad car right now."

All my pleas fall on deaf ears as the chief takes me to the station in his car. He locks me in the hold-up. With no lights, only the full moonlight beams into the rearview area window. I keep asking why. He says, "You're lucky. Now sober up. See you in the morning."

CHAPTER 15

Discovering the Corpses

I SIT IN THIS COLD ROOM, WITH MICE RUNNING IN AND out of the cell, sometimes under me while at other times right beside me. A pale, yellow bulb flickers in the center of the cell. I look around and notice the rusty bars of the prison surrounding me. Half-drunk, half-sober, I try to comprehend the situation that I find myself in.

Suddenly, the same woman from the bar wearing the same short leather dress with dark, red lipstick sits across me in the jail cell. Wait a second. I pinch myself and look around, "What the hell is this?" I murmur.

"You read too much, ask too many questions, you're just a very natty old man. Tch tch tch, shame on you," says the barwoman.

I must admit looking at her gave me a huge erection, but I quickly lost it because none of this made sense to me. The barwoman sat next to me. Her pale skin, red lips, fingernails become more visible. Wearing an intoxicating perfume, she kisses me on the lips and drops a book in my lap. Within seconds, the texture of her voice changes. Her enticing, sweet, feminine voice changes into a manly one, saying:

"Finish writing my story, professor."

* * *

When I open up my eyes, I hear keys clacking. Someone whistles and walks up to my holding cell. I realize it's the chief. "Well, well, from the sound of your loud ass snoring, you know you should see a doctor and take care of that sleep. Apnea can kill you, you know. Anyway, you had a good night's sleep, so I'm gonna let you go home this morning. Plus, I got a call from the local landfill about some corpse. Lucky for you, I hate damn paperwork. So, go home, professor," says the police chief.

I grab my jacket and shake it. A mouse falls out of the arm sleeve. Then a police officer hands me my personal items. Just like that, I walk out of the Palmyra police station and call a transportation service to drive me home.

Meanwhile, the chief drives off toward Palmyra County land-fill; the city and county's names are the same. As he drives up to the office, two men in black suits and white shirts, black sunglasses, and ties walk toward his squad car. The chief, about to park, peeps over his aviator sunglasses. After parking the car, he steps out and pulls up his police belt.

"Damn, fellas, I know I'm well liked around these parts, but didn't know like this." Then after a brief pause, he continues, "From the looks of you fellas, you must be from corporate. What's this I hear about the corpse?"

One of the guys in a suit points the chief in the direction of an arriving black Ford pickup. Everyone gets inside it. They drive through a guard shack with and an electric gate and straight inside the landfill. Bumping side to side while traveling the route, the truck finally stops. As the officers come out of the vehicle, their shoes and boots touch down on brown dirt as loose white papers swirl around their feet. They walk over to a roped-off section and notice black crows flying around in circles, up in the sky. They walk up, show-ing the chief three separate areas where human corpses are cut open from the Adam's apple down to their genitals, nothing inside but pieces of landfill trash. A breeze picks up, sending pieces of land-fill debris on the chief and guys in black. Then one of them, named

Harry, speaks up, "What you're looking at needs to stay here. If word gets out, the county commission will not let us expand, and as you know, one of those commissioners owns the Palmyra newspaper. Ariel will not vote. We need a majority."

The chief looks around, pulling up his police belt. He sucks his teeth and then scratches one of his long Elvis Presley sideburns. "Well, fellas, looks like you got yourselves in one hell of a mess. Be careful, so we don't all find ourselves in the Fed Pen. I'm going to need to take pictures, identify the bodies, notify the next of kin."

Then the chief continues, "As far as I'm concerned, I never was here, which means I need the security footage. You folks call someone not associated with this place to pick up bodies found in a dumpster before they arrive here!"

The chief storms off, and the two guys run after him, calling for him to stop. Dust and landfill debris swirl in his face. The large, black crow birds fly overhead. Guys in black suits hop in their black SUV, driving alongside the chief. Harry puts his head out the window, pleading for him to get in. By this time, the chief is completely covered in dust. He gets in his police car and peels off, leaving a cloud of dust behind him in the parking lot.

* * *

BANG, BANG.

"That's not bad, momma. Daddy would be proud of your catch," says Amy, Ariel's daughter, happily. The two walk through a wooded wild turkey hunting area, hunting during the spring season. After catching two nearly 25-pound turkeys, they stop to take a selfie of their catch while sitting on a large fallen tree. Their beagle hunting dog, Charm, runs up to them with a human heart in its mouth.

"Charm, what is that? Put it down!" The obedient dog puts it on the ground and begins wagging her tail, barking. Then running in a certain direction for a short distance she comes back to Ariel and her daughter as if asking them to follow her. Both the mother and daughter look at each other. Then the two put their dead turkeys in their backpacks and walk in the direction of Charm.

While following the beagle, Ariel stumbles on the ground. As she gets up, she notices she is covered in blood. "Oh my God! Amy, help me! Am I shot? Look at all this blood and gooey stuff on me! Help me wipe it off, Amy. Hurry up!"

"Momma, what is this?" inquires Amy, somewhat in a shock.

They look down and notice numerous mounds around them. Using fallen thick tree branches, they dig and pull the human remains of guts, intestines, lungs, hearts, and more. Amy, who is a medical doctor herself, immediately recognizes the parts as human remains.

Walking back to their pickup truck with her blood-soaked mother smelling like rotten eggs, Amy calls the chief. As soon as he picks up, she blurts out, "Get over to the Palmyra turkey hunting reserve. You are not going to believe this!"

The chief, still in the vicinity, makes a quick U-turn. The blue and red lights of his car flicker as he hits his siren, speeding up to nearly 80 miles per hour on the county highway. He pulls into the hunting entrance and, looking at his GPS, drives directly over to where the women are walking toward their pickup truck.

Ariel says to the chief, "I'll walk to the truck to clean my blood-soaked clothes. In the meantime, you, along with my daughter, walk to the grave spots." Without any delay, the two walk toward the same area. They notice the whole place is soggy, oozing a green and red substance. When the chief's boots touch the ground, he says, "Well, well, looks like someone has dug graves for human guts. Get Ariel back home safely. Let me handle this. I'll have some of my ranch hands clean this up. A word about this sick and disgusting scene will stop that new meatpacking plant from coming to the city."

"I'll tell momma not to put this in the paper. You're right, not a good look for the town," says Amy thoughtfully. Then she says, "I heard about the missing kid at the school. How did it happen?"

"Seems like all hell is breaking loose in this town. Come by my place for drinks tonight. Bring Chinese too. I'll bring you up to speed," says the chief with a wink.

The chief dials his mobile phone as he walks around the soggy shallow remains of graves. Eyes fixed on the ground, he notices a consistent pattern of dog paw prints and identical nail scratches in front of all four shallow graves. "Don't tell me, no, no way!" Then, on the phone, he says, "Hey Leo, round up the boys from the ranch, bring a back loader, telescopic bobcat handler, the dump truck sawdust, and hay. Also, going to need about 10 workers."

Bright equipment lights on top of heavy equipment rolled into the wooded turkey hunting area. Wide tread wheels squishing mud and human remains, digging and dumping human guts now liquified onto sawdust and hay at the bottom of a large dump truck. The smell has workers coughing some vomit as their hard hat lights shine on the gruesome death scene. Black bats fly above the working area treetops, flying above the night's horizon. Workers hear the creatures' wings flapping.

Most workers show drenching perspiration into their goggles and onto their clothes. "Oh, help me, somebody help me," screams one of the workers who falls from the back of the pickup truck into a grave still full of human organs. Everyone runs over to help him. The worker is screaming, now waste high. He throws off his hat and starts pulling off his shirt, "Something is eating me! Something is eating me!" screams the worker repeatedly. They throw a large rope with a noose and tell him to put it under his armpits. A pickup truck has the other end attached and starts pulling the worker out of the ground, "Come on, you can do it! We're here with you! Come on!" scream the workers.

Looking over at the driver of the pickup truck, the chief cusses. Then he quickly runs over to the truck and pulls out the driver. The chief starts maneuvering the truck in a different direction. That's when the rope snaps the worker's armpits and wraps around his neck, leaving his body to melt into the mud with the rest of the human organs. His head is still out of the ground, allowing him to scream in pain. Panicked, everyone starts running in the woods. The chief quickly hops out of the truck, pulls up his pants, and fires two shots, one in the air. Everyone stops and walks back only to witness the chief fire a single bullet between the eyes of the head of the screaming worker. Nearly out of breath, he retorts, "Now I'm not paying you folks to plant a garden, so let's get it finished and follow me to the landfill. I got a date tonight, and this needs to be done soon."

Bats fly away. Two hours later, the dump truck pulls up to the landfill guard gate and drives away, disappearing into the dusty compound hills. An hour later, the chief, now waiting at the guard gate, inspects the truck and waves the driver past the gate.

* * *

The garage door opens, and the chief picks up truck parts. His muddy black boots click on the concrete floor, and the door is closed. The chief walks into his kitchen from the garage.

"Well, I was thinking you were going to stand me up in your own house. It's past 10 p.m. That took a long time," says Amy with a grin.

"Well, yeah, pour me four shots of whiskey and a couple of those California gummy bears for this one," says the chief. He takes his gun holster off and puts away his .45 in the kitchen cabinet, takes off his clothes now, and butt naked walks them over to his washer.

"Chief, you need to work on those love handles. Besides, I'm 15 years younger than you. I'm too young to see your naked ass. Go take a shower," says Ariel's daughter. Testicles swinging, the chief walks over to the kitchen counter. He picks up his shot of whisky and then eats two California gummy bears. "When I get back, I want you in one of my silk robes hanging up in the laundry room."

With the running water flowing from the showerhead, the chief steps inside the bathroom. As he shampoos his hair, and scrubs his body, the bathroom light flickers. The chief steps out, dries off, and steps to the toilet to take a leak. He sees a small black bat in his toilet and jumps back, dribbling the last remains of pee on his bathroom floor.

"Hey, big guy, what's taking so long? I'm here waiting for you. Get down here now," says Amy.

"Aww, yeah, babe," replies the chief.

On the way to her, he looks in the mirror and says to himself, "This is why I preach just say no to drugs." He flushes the toilet, puts on his robe and slippers, and walks out, going downstairs. Totally horny, he is unaware the bat was real and that he did not flush it down the toilet. As he walks down the stairs, the bat slowly floats on top.

The chief walks over to Amy and takes another shot and some more California gummies. "So, Ariel is all recovered from the day."

"Yeah. Anyway, what the hell took you so long? I was starting to get worried."

"Well, it was a gross mess. We dumped it in the landfill with the cut-up corpses I found earlier in the day," replies the Chief.

"Get over hee,r chief. You know how to turn me on," she pushes the chief gently on the couch and gets on her knees, licking his private parts. Then she mounts him as he grabs her waist and her long blond hair falls on his face. Amy moans and does he as they kiss passionately. He squeezes her nipples, and they get louder and louder, breathing intensely. She takes her top off, her breasts bouncing up and down. She keeps moaning and groaning louder and louder as her passion and intensity increase.

Just as they climax, water drips on top of them. The bat and water rain on their organs. "Oh shit, Oh shit!" says Amy. Looking up at the ceiling, she sees water everywhere. The bat flaps its wings in the water. "Get back!" shouts the chief, running toward the kitchen cabinet and grabbing his gun.

Amy tries to run but falls on the bat, screaming and crying. The chief rolls her off and fires. *BANG, BANG.* Shoots the bat dead, or so it appears.

"You okay? Come on, Amy, get up. I'm driving you to the hospital. There are clean towels in the dryer."

The chief and Amy drive off to the hospital around 2 a.m. She gets a shot, and the two check into a hotel for the night.

CHAPTER 16

Last Stand at the Palmyra High School

ALEX RUNS LIKE THE WIND WITH HIS TWO REMAINING friends—Marie and Amelio. Breathless and panting nonstop, the three friends run down the hall and keep moving forward with a deep sense of sadness slowly lurking over their bosom. Leaving their dearest friend Brandon behind at the mercy of the ghost was something none of them had wanted or even thought of. And the possibility of their friend being the next victim just broke their hearts.

When Alex finally stops in one dark corner of a classroom, Marie and Amelio come to a halt, too. All of them are equally saddened, thinking about the fate of Brandon. Looking at Amelio and Marie, Alex musters up his courage and finally speaks up, "I know how horrible you both feel on the inside because I feel that, too. But please understand that there was nothing any of us could have done considering the circumstances."

While stopping by to get a breather and regrouping his thoughts, Alex goes on to say, "Please, guys, hold yourself up. We cannot lose hope at this point. I know all this is difficult, but…" Alex stops speaking as if unable to carry on with his false sense of security. All the stress has Alex on edge. While sitting at a student desk, he lays his head down so the veins in his head can stop pulsating uncontrollably in his forehead.

Amelio and Marie close the classroom door behind them. Marie stays by the door and keeps watch, peeking through the small window in the door. Amelio walks up and whispers tiredly, "What's going to be our next move, Alex? Is there even an end to this nightmare?"

Alex tries putting a positive spin on the situation, even though part of his brain is losing hope with each passing second. "I'm sick from all of our friends dying," Alex tells everyone. "It is true that I feel the weight of all this really breaking me down physically as well as mentally. And honestly, I am also uncertain of the possibility of carrying out our plan of burning the building and killing the ghost successfully. I keep wondering what will happen if our plan is a dud; what if it doesn't work? What if we're just setting ourselves up to get killed out of a burning building?" Then after a pause, he resumes, "What if we are wrong about the ghost dying in the building and his connection with the school? What would happen if this monster's spirit comes back after the school is rebuilt?" Alex asks everyone.

After listening to Alex's what-ifs and maybes, Marie speaks up, this time confidently, "Alex, will you please stop being so negative? Now is not the time for all this talk. We need to have faith in ourselves and our strategy." Reassuring all of them that the plan is going to work, she continues, "We can defeat this monster, guys, and we surely will!"

At that moment, Alex could see the commitment and strong character of Cassandra, Marie's mother, reflected in the girl as well. Her mother, a psychic, is a strong, confident woman who is very well aware of what she is doing. Alex had known her because of his friendship with Marie ever since he was a kid. He begins reminiscing about the good old days when they'd get into trouble for going through the part of their house that was off-limits because of the presence of her mom's candles, sage raps, salt, statues, and these strange-looking over-sided cards lying on a red cloth table.

Interrupting Alex's thoughts, Marie tells her friends, "The ghost in this Palmyra High School acts like a ghost that has not come to closure with leaving Earth. I feel like he's probably in purgatory, not ready to crossover."

"Yeah, like I said from my web searches, a janitor died in this building from a heart attack," says Alex. With that, Marie continues to share the information regarding deaths and spirits that she is aware of because of her mother. Marie tells them about the ghost trying to cling to Earth's gravitational pull and how this ghost is probably confused or upset by the way he died in this building. Then she adds, "I could be wrong, but this spirit looks as though he is gaining power based on his red eyes, his ability to morph through walls, and the fact that he takes on a half-human ghostly creature image at any time."

"And what do you think about our plan of burning this building down? Do you think that would work in our favor?" asks Amelio.

Marie answers confidently, "Burning the building with him in it may be the best idea because the school is now his home."

Nodding his head, Amelio says, "Maybe you're right. The move is going to save the town of Palmyra. But how can you be so confident about all these details regarding the ghost's spirit and purgatory, Marie?"

"To be honest, my mom had asked me not to leave the house for the camping trip we'd planned earlier. She had warned me that I would be encountering a very evil spirit. In fact, my mother put a temporary red X tattoo on the back of my neck," Marie said while showing them the small X. "I had to agree to this mark or would have been grounded, unable to leave the house. It's going to only last six months, so I guess I'm immune to the forces of evil."

"Why didn't you listen to her when you know she is aware of information that is hidden from others?" Alex asked concernedly.

"Guys, at the time, I thought she was crazy, being too extreme and all. I mean, the cards, candles, and seance were hokey, the X was really over the top, but this shit we just experienced I'm glad my mama is my mona cause I know she's feeling me, so let's get it on. Let's kill the ghost and get rid of him for once and all."

"Okay," Alex says, "Sounds like the best means to kill a ghost is fire."

"Yes. Based on my mom's teachings, I would say fire is one of the best avenues of getting rid of a ghost," says Marie. She then explains the difference between burning the actual ghost and burning where the ghost gets his energy source. "If we burn just the ghost, he's going to weaken only to regenerate. We must burn the source, bones, and the ghost's last living attachment—the Palmyra High School," says Marie. "Like Brandon said before he was murdered, the ghost cleans up his mess, fixes any damages, knows how to control the doors and power of the school," continues Marie.

"I agree it all makes sense," Alex says thoughtfully while scratching his head, still frustrated and a bit confused. Then he concludes, "If I set the ghost on fire, it can harm the ghost. As the school burns, the ghost burns and dies. His spirit will then go away in smoke, and his physical ghost body turns into ashes."

"Yup, that simple. My mom knows her stuff, so let's stop talking and get to the action right away. We don't have a lot of time. I feel tensed, though. It seems as if my heart will come out of my chest any second," says Marie.

"Yeah, mine too," mumbles Amelio.

"All right, guys. Let's do it!" Alex says getting up from his desk. He digs in his bag full of cleaning chemical products and grabs the flammable ones first. He starts searching for some type of glass bottle around the classroom. Luckily, his eyes land on a science project with a Coke bottle on its display. Ripping it from the display, he cracks open the chemicals, pouring them in the bottle halfway. Once that's done, he starts searching around the classroom, this time looking for a rag. As soon as he finds it, he stuffs it in the Coke bottle. Soon, it starts soaking the chemicals poured previously.

"Dude, what are you doing?" asks Amelio.

"I'm making a Molotov to throw at the ghost when the time presents itself," Alex tells Amelio. Once that is done, he says, "All right, now listen carefully. There are two science labs in the back. One goes through the gym, it's a good shortcut, and I'm hoping we get there quicker than the second option, which is straight through, but the entrance is on the opposite side of the lab. Both rooms have gas burners and also have flammable chemicals that we can pour throughout the halls. I believe this will help us expedite the spreading of the fire."

Everyone looks at Alex with their jaws widened. Alex continues saying, "Once we start the fire, hot flames are going to dance across the floor into the science labs and blow from butane gas build-up. Then we're going to the kitchen and turn those burners on as well."

After a brief pause, Alex asks Amelio and Marie, "Everyone ready?"

Amelio shows a thumbs-up sign while Marie nods. They take a deep breath and, accepting the fate of their challenge, begin preparing for their attack. Leaving the classroom, Amelio toting a bag of cleaning chemicals, Marie carrying a large wooden broom with plastic sweepers, they pray silently to be successful in their mission. Alex holds the little fire bomb with a lighter in his top pocket, fully prepared to light up the dark ghost.

They are all ready for anything and everything. Trembling in fear, they feel an adrenaline rush through their bodies. Their hearts beat faster, and sweat covers their faces. Blocking out feelings of hunger, pain, and exhaustion, they grit their teeth while finding a way to mentally and physically end the madness. Tiptoeing down the halls, they head to the science rooms.

Four of our friends are dead; they didn't deserve any of this madness. All they were trying to do was to find our friend who went missing, thinks Alex to himself. *If the ghost wants to play games, we're prepared to fight with fire, literally even if it kills us.*

Creeping through the halls, they get closer to the gym.

"All this feels so weird right now," whispers Alex as a sinking feeling moves around the lower end of his stomach.

"I feel like we're being watched," Amelio murmurs back as he feels the hairs on his arms and neck pull his skin stick straight up.

It's awfully quiet in the building, so much so that they can even hear spiders crawling in the vents—a bad sign. *I kind of wish the ghost would just do something already*, thinks Alex.

The trio feels like they were playing Russian roulette with the ghost, not knowing what corner or what spot the ghost is going to spring from or which wall or floor he will morph through. They approach the double gym doors, and, slowly pushing them open, they peek around. It's dark and quiet; nothing could be seen or heard, just an empty gym. The exit door is on the other side of the gym. Alex, Amelio, and Marie stop halfway across the gym. Their exit door is rusty, squealing slowly, they begin opening it. But just then, a dominating shadowy figure moves across their bodies, and like a reflex, everyone steps back. The room grows colder, and basketball rims, along with the rest of the gym equipment, start rattling.

Within seconds, the ghost figure appears out of nowhere and starts to charge at Alex and his friends. They take off running and dash into the locker rooms that were on the side of the gym. Through the door, they go to the back of the locker rooms, hiding around the corner.

Everyone is trapped in the locker rooms. "The ghost must have stopped running after us. He'd been in the room by now," whispers Alex. Then he gets ready, wasting no time in adjusting his home-made bomb, ready to throw it at any second. Lighter in one hand and the cocktail bomb in the other hand, Alex is absolutely ready to end the chaos. He notices some baseball bats near them, grabs a few, tossing some to Amelio and Marie, telling them to stay alert.

Seconds later, eerie sounds vibrate throughout the walls echoing locker room doors slowly opening, old hinges squeaking. Heavy footsteps pound the concrete floor; it sounds like the ghost is on the right side of Alex's body. Getting closer, Alex flicks his lighter, ready to light the chemical-soaked rag. He patiently waits for the footsteps to move closer. Then giving the others the eye, he jumps out of the corner and aims to throw a fastball. Alex pauses midway, and sliding back into the corner realizes that the ghost is not there. Alex immediately signals to the others, indicating that it's just a false alarm.

Sweating excessively and panicking, Alex begins looking around. He was 100 per cent sure that the ghostly apparition was just in the room. Where could he have possibly disappeared?

"Somebody help me please!" screams Marie, interrupting Alex's thoughts. The ghost grabs her and throws her frail frame across the locker room. Her body slams right into several lockers, eventually falling to the floor.

Amelio tries hiding behind Alex. The ghost turns his head, displaying his bright bloodshot eyes. He charges toward them, morphing into a part-human and part-ghost creature.

Reacting quickly, Alex remembers he still has the Molotov cocktail. Without giving it a second thought, he lights it and throws it at the ghost, thinking it'll explode in his face. The ghost falls back into the lockers and, using his skinny, stringy ghost arms and hands, tries to put out the fire. Ashes and smoke burn into the air as the ghost burns down to a pile of fine black coal pieces, his ghostly spirit disappearing.

Alex and Amelio are relieved, watching the ghost dissolve into small chunks of black bones. They run past the burning coal and rush over to Marie. Shaking her body, they try to wake her up from being knocked out. She slowly comes to her consciousness. Both the boys help her up, attempting to exit the locker room. The locker room doors begin banging loud and fast—the movement and the sound are deafening, out of control.

They rush out of the locker room back into the gym, heading to the door leading to the science room. Going through the door, they

Terrell Newby

stop in the middle of the halls, letting Marie catch her breath. Every now and then, they look back to see if anything or perhaps anyone is behind them while simultaneously reminding Marie that staying too long in one spot is not best and that they've got to keep moving.

Seconds later, they hear loud animal grunt breathing and the sound "click, clacking," walking, coming in their direction. Marie knows they can't stay much longer. The thundering footsteps of the animal walking toward them ring in their ears. Behind them at the gym doors, an enormous dog brown with a silk short hair coat, pointed nose, tall ears, rust color above his eyes and under his neck appears. The dog takes a seat at attention, staring at the three teens with olive-shaped red glowing eyes.

"Ah, guys, where did the dog come from?" asks Amelio frightfully. Alex and Marie shrug their shoulders, not knowing where it came from. But they don't stand around to find out. In fact, the three begin walking away from it. Showing his teeth with white saliva dripping between his pearly white razor-sharp canine teeth onto the ground, the dog stands up on all fours and then on his two hind legs, barking at them slowly. Walking toward them like a human being, it looks as though the dog is going to attack. As Alex and his friends begin to walk faster, picking up their pace, the dog bellows a loud roar, somewhat like the sound of a Viking horn. One leap, and the

246

dog is airborne, heading straight in their direction. He charges full force toward them as they continue to run to the science room down the hall. The dog continues barking and howling, his long nails clicking on the floor.

Alex, Marie, and Amelio feel the science room getting closer with each strike of their feet hitting the floor. They run so hard and slide into the science room that their breathing gets affected. Once inside, Amelio slams the door. Coughing, bending over, and catching their breath, they hear the dog slamming his body into the door on his hind legs. They hear the creature scratching, barking, growling like a beast ready to attack.

Although relieved to be where they wanted to be, that is, in the science room, they are confused, thinking about how to get out because of this crazed dog present right outside of this door.

"What now?" Marie says in a panicking tone. "I don't know. Staying here is not a good idea," Alex replies while gathering his breath from once again running for his life in this school.

A few minutes pass by before Amelio speaks up, "Listen. It's quiet now. The dog must have gone. We've got to get out before I go crazy! Don't know how much more of this madness I can take, guys."

"He is right. It is quiet indeed. I think it's time to move ahead," says Marie. Amelio, standing close to the door, looks out the window and sees the dog sitting at attention, waiting for them to come out of the room.

"This is crazy! Whoever heard of a ghost having a pet dog, what's next?" says Amelio out of frustration. Amelio walks to the other side of the room, putting his head down as if losing all hopes of the plan.

Everyone just feels despondent. Analyzing the situation, Alex says, "Guys, I know it is tough, but we need to stay positive. It is times like these that decide what we're really capable of." He goes on to say, "I've got an idea that just might get us in the clear. Remember, before we open the door just stick to our original plan. Open all the gas burners, gather more flammable liquids." "But what about the dog?" asks Marie.

"We are going to let the dog in the room -," replies Alex.

"What? Are you crazy, like out of your mind dude, or what? No way are we gonna do anything like that!" argues Amelio.

"I didn't complete my sentence, Amelio. At least give me a chance to explain the next plan. Will you?"

When Amelio nods, Alex continues, "We let the dog in, and you, Amelio, clobber it on the head with the bat so hard, it knocks the fleabag out of him. Then run out of the room, lock him in here with the gas on. When gas from the burners is on, the fumes will kill the dog and keep him from waking up anymore," Alex explains.

"We're ready, open the door," says Marie.

Amelio looks outside and sees the dog is sitting at attention like a statue waiting.

"Okay good," responds Alex. Amelio gets ready with his bat while Marie stands on the other side of the door with a broomstick she found in the classroom. Alex points with his fingers to three, and on three, he signals with his fist to stop. Alex asks one more time, "Is everybody ready?" Both Marie and Amelio nod yes. Alex counts to three and yanks the door open. The first person the dog lands his red eyes on is Amelio. Walking on two hind legs straight like a human, he keeps looking at Amelio with his mouth open and saliva falling on the floor. The dog keeps barking uncontrollably, and their ears ring from the loud sounds. Terrified of the animal, Amelio falls backward, giving the dog the chance to jump on top of him. The possessed creature starts biting his arm, trying to rip it off.

Alex grabs Marie's stick and starts beating the dog with it, but that doesn't work. It only makes the dog angrier. It charges at Alex, jumping on top of him and trying to bite him. But Alex is not one to surrender. He catches the dog's teeth in the broomstick and attempts to keep him off. The dog is super strong, too. He snaps the stick in half and eats the remaining wood in his teeth. *Boom!* Out of nowhere, Amelio hits a home run on the side of the dog's head. The dog falls to the floor, twitching with foam coming from his mouth.

Amelio helps Alex get right up off the floor, and the three rush out of the science room. Right behind them, the dog gets right up and starts to chase them. Just in time, Marie slams the door right in the dog's face. But that didn't stop the dog. He continues scratching at the door, barking, slamming his body against the door, determined to break through the barrier to his prey.

Without wasting any time, Alex, Marie, and Amelio run to the other science room to do the same thing. Once done, they pour all the chemicals all over the carpet floor in the second science room to the hallways so the fire would travel to the room and catch bigger flames. Alex lights some paper towels on fire, dropping them on the soaked wooden floor. Within seconds, huge flames rise, dancing into the classroom. Not looking back, all they can see is the light from the fire reflected off the walls from behind them. Running past the other science room, Alex takes a quick peek in the room and sees the dog lying dead on the floor from being in the gas-trapped room. Moving quickly before the gas-filled room explodes, Alex can smell gas seeping through the cracks in the door, going into the halls.

Soon, that will catch fire and blow up, thinks Alex.

One corner of the school is already on fire, moving fast down the hallway and spreading from room to room. They hear the wood cracking and popping. Everything is going according to the plan. Smoke and flames dominate the school halls—a contrast of yellow flames reflecting off of dark smoke, advancing as the heat melts the lockers.

"This is good now," murmurs Alex. "The ghost can't stop the fire because if he could, it would have been done by now."

CHAPTER 17

The Horrors of Inferno

WITHIN MINUTES, THE FIRE BEGINS TO CATCH SPEED. The mighty flames start to spread far and wide, into the corridors and then the classrooms, one at a time. It is hard to ignore the glowing bright orange and yellow blaze in contrast with the school walls' dull background. It ignites whatever it touches, like a vengeful assassin destroying whatever comes in its way. As the classroom desks go up in flames, the heat within the building multiplies, making it difficult for any human to stay inside the premises.

"Once the flames hit the other science room, it is over for the ghost," says Marie to her friends hopefully.

With his shirt drenched in sweat, Alex nods and replies, "Guys, we need to rush to the entrance and see if we can escape from there. The last thing we want is to get left in flames and burn to death."

Without any further discussion, the trio begins to head toward the main entrance of the school. All three of them want to see if the doors open up, letting them escape from this nightmare and the burning school. Sprinting through the gym and out the other side back into the dark halls, they keep hoping and praying for a miracle. Alex notices the lockers in the locker room going out of control, opening and shutting repeatedly. Everything around them seems to be going crazy. They see papers hovering in the air, books, and binders flying out of the lockers as if trying to hit them on someone's orders. Even the constant fluctuation of lights makes it difficult for them to see things clearly. Dipping and dodging through everything, they finally manage to come out and almost reach the main entrance.

But there's one more door to go through. Just one more door to freedom.

Just as they reach for the doorknob, the door slams shut right in Amelio's face, breaking his nose on the wooden door. Blood rushes out of his nose as he gets up and snaps it back in place. Screaming because of the pain, he uses his shirt and plugs his nose, trying his best to stop the blood from oozing. Alex wishes to tend to his friend's injury, but doesn't know how to do it. He just stays there, saying words of motivation to make his friend feel better. "Try looking up at the ceiling, Amelio. That might stop the bleeding. Dude, you need to stay strong! It'll all be okay. Hang in there."

Just then, a cloud of black smoke due to the fire behind them rushes in their direction. They immediately try to open the door, but just as before, it's locked.

"We can't go back because of the smoke, and we can't go forward because of this stupid gate! We are basically trapped between the cloud of smoke and a locked door. What do we do now, Alex?" shouts Marie, her tired eyes looking from Alex to Amelio, who is holding his injured nose.

Alex begins banging and kicking the door, and Marie follows suit. The smoke gets closer and closer, but they keep beating at the door as if taking out their frustration and annoyance on a non-living object. Losing time and nowhere to go because of the dark smoke right behind them, they feel stuck.

That's when their worst nightmare comes true.

The same monster, changing its form from the ghostly shadowy figure to a vile half-human creature, rushes out of the smoke and charges right at Alex and his friends. It grabs Marie and Alex by their throats and violently kicks Amelio to the ground, putting his big foot on top of his face and pinning him down to the floor. Amelio's arms continue flapping like a fish out of water. He keeps twisting his head side to side screaming and choking as his injured nose bleeds further.

Fog smoke fills the area, and the three friends barely struggle to breathe. Because of the lack of oxygen and the powerful black fumes, everyone is about to pass out. Everything starts going black because of the smoke. At this point, the trio is unable to get any visual or see anyone in front of them. They are moments away from completely blacking out when they hear a loud *boom*. A massive explosion behind them lights up the room momentarily.

Because of the explosion, the ghost drops Alex and Marie and takes his foot off Amelio's face. All three look up only to see a quickly moving yellow and red fireball coming in their direction. Unscathed, the ghost stands there. Alex, Amelio, and Marie turn their faces down and, covering their heads with their hands, prepare themselves for the impact of the shock wave coming in their direction.

Boom! The fireball hits the ghost.

The trio hears him zoom past them in the air with the fireball. The ghostly figure flies through the locked door that had trapped the three friends in the smoke. The other science room finally catches fire, exploding into pieces. Somehow, the trio lucked out because of them laying on the floor several inches below the blast wave. Looking around up is an open door. With no hesitation, the three teenagers run out of the smoke-filled hall.

By this time, the fire is roaring through the entire back half of the school. The blaze continues to spread quickly, igniting all the objects in its way. Running as fast as they could, they finally make it to the main entrance. In front of them are the doors leading to their escape. "I'm pretty sure these doors are locked as well," says Amelio, somewhat disheartened.

But that doesn't stop them from reaching the gates. Running full speed, they all crash into the doors, bouncing off into the air and landing ten feet away from the exit on the floor. Desperately trying to open the door again, they once again start pushing and pulling. But much to their dismay, nothing works. They bang on the surface and then slam their bodies against the glass door multiple times, but it doesn't break at all, leaving them still trapped in the burning building.

"I thought the ghost wouldn't have control over the building anymore," Amelio shouts to Marie.

"What are you shouting at me for? How was I supposed to know this wouldn't work?" Marie replies, equally frustrated. They two begin pushing and shoving each other, arguing about why the plan is not working.

Alex has to get in the middle to break up the rising tension. "Guys! Please! Will you two stops acting like kids? We are so close to our freedom, and this is how you both behave?"

While Alex lectures Amelio and Marie for their childish behavior, they hear someone banging on the glass doors behind them. Startled, they all turn around to see who it was and set eyes on the last person they'd expected to see outside of the school.

Crazy as it sounds, it was D'Angelo.

"I can't believe this. The guy I knocked out earlier with a bat is looking at us in our time of need," whispers Alex as if in a shock.

Several thoughts come into Alex's mind as he sees his friend's face outside the glass door. *Could this really be D'Angelo, or is the ghost playing some last-minute dirty trick on us?* he thinks to himself.

As they are looking at D'Angelo in absolute shock, they notice he is trying to tell them something. But because of all the chaos, they are unable to grasp what their friend is trying to say. Alex points at his ears, attempting to tell D'Angelo that they can't hear him. D'Angelo starts jumping up and down in the air, starts pointing right behind Alex and his friends, looking like he's about to have a panic attack. The three friends turn around and see the ghost coming right for them. Without giving it a second thought, they all split up and end up going in three different ways, thinking the ghost can only chase one of them. This way, there's some chance of surviving.

Unfortunately, the floor moves as the ghost chases after Alex. With that, at least one thing becomes clear; D'Angelo is real, and it's not some sort of a trick.

Alex runs his ass off straight into the kitchen and tries to hide around the corner by some gas stoves. The ghost appears behind him. All of a sudden, he stops in his tracks and looks around, his blood-red eyes searching for Alex. A wicked grin spreads across the ghost's countenance as he spots his next target. In a flash, he charges at Alex, jumping over the middle counter toward his face. Alex quickly jumps out of the way, and the ghost ends up throwing his body over the gas stove. It breaks the gas line that emerges from the ground to the stove.

Terrified and shaking, Alex gets up, trying to escape the ghost but too late. He falls to the ground after the ghost grabs his leg. Alex starts kicking and shaking his leg. When that doesn't work, he begins moving his entire body with all his strength, but nothing stops the ghost from wreaking havoc. The ghost slowly gets up. Now Alex is hanging upside-down by the leg. The pungent smell of the gas, now filling the kitchen, hits Alex's nose.

Unaware, the ghost swings Alex back and forth, hitting him against the wall ruthlessly and sliding him across the kitchen table. While moving like a pendulum from one side to the other, Alex's eyes are caught by a glistening object lying in one corner of the table. It's a knife stand with several big, and small knives tucked in it. The moment Alex gets near it, he grabs one large knife. Its sharp, pointy edge, shining strikingly, gives him hope.

The ghost continues slinging Alex back and forth like a rag doll. Gradually, his face turns blood-red. Looking down at the floor being twirled, he tries gasping for air. Just as Alex is about to pass out, he musters up courage as an adrenaline rush hits him. Thinking of it as perhaps his last attempt, he lifts his upper body up and, with all his might, stabs the ghostly creature in his fragile-looking arm with the help of the knife he had got hold of earlier.

Thud. Alex drops to the floor.

With the same knife, Alex stabs the ghost again and then again, in the same arm, very much relieved to hear the ghost screaming in pain.

Knowing that he has to leave the spot immediately, Alex takes off running. Although in excruciating pain himself, with his nose and mouth bleeding, he doesn't lose hope. Flames meet him right when he reaches for the exit door. He sees a huge fireball heading his way. Behind him, the half-human ghost is struggling with the knife, pulling it slowly out of his arm.

As Alex looks in the front, scared by the sheer size of the fireball, something else catches his attention. He sees the same dog, this time behind the fireball, and his eyes widen with fear. Their eyes connect, and within seconds, the dog comes flying through the fireball straight for Alex's face. "Oh. Shit! Help!" Alex is being tackled by the dog, its body engulfed in flames. Alex ducks just in the nick of time as the flaming dog flies into the gas-filled kitchen with the ghost in it.

Alex gets up and, slamming the door behind, takes off running. *Boom!* The room blows up with Alex just a few feet away from the kitchen. Because of the explosion, the door comes flying off the hinges. Alex's head starts ringing from the shockwave of the explosion, causing him to black out. Stretched out on the floor, with tiny glass and wood chips in his back, he lays unconscious.

Moments pass by before Alex's double vision starts coming into focus, looking at and hearing Marie and Amelio shouting, shaking, and slapping him in the face to wake up. They almost knocked him out again, hitting his back and slapping him so that he gains consciousness.

"Ouch! Stop it, guys! It hurts," mutters Alex.

"Oh, thank god you're all right! You just scared the hell out of me," says Marie, hugging Alex with tears in her worried eyes.

Flames continue surrounding them slowly. It seems as if the entire school is in flames. Part of the ceiling is gone as Alex looks above him at the blue skies. Then he sees the door open, and his eyes just lighten up. The three of them struggle to get out, slipping on glass and debris every now and then. Marie and Amelio try to help Alex walk out. Then they see D'Angelo. He grabs Alex and, throwing his body over his shoulders, runs out of the burning building. Marie and Amelio follow them, and the group finally reach the car.

D'Angelo throws Alex in the back seat of the car, and they burn rubber down the road. Right behind them, the sky lights up super bright. The school just explodes into a million pieces. Alex rubs his head, crying happy tears. "I can't believe we're finally out of that hell-house. But how did we do that? The last thing I remember was closing the door on the ghost with the flaming dog, and that's really it. But how did we escape?" Alex asked.

Amelio explained what happened. "When you closed the door, it came off its hinges with the explosion. That door flew off, zooming through the entrance doors violently. It shattered the glass in all directions, sticking in the ceiling, walls, and floors. This was pretty much the time you lay unconscious on the floor, dude." Then after a while, he continues, "Dude, honestly, when I saw you lying on the floor, I thought you were dead for a minute. Marie thought the same and began freaking out."

Alex looks toward Marie and smiles gently. He was moved to see that she still cared for him.

Everyone glances back at the school, watching it burn, hearing small explosions every now and then. Then they focus on the road in front of them, never looking back again.

"Where to now, guys?" asks D'Angelo.

"Well, we are supposed to be on vacation camping for spring break, aren't we? I'm texting for the location now," says Alex.

"I agree! Let's go. I need a vacation after all this nightmare," says Marie.

The group heads off to the campsite to finish their spring break. After all the pain and trauma, they endured, camping sounded like a beautiful thing they felt they deserved. And although the grief of losing their friends will remain within their hearts forever, they realized they had to move on with their lives—the sooner, the better.

CHAPTER 18

Ariel's Contemplation

AFTER LISTENING TO BISHOP FAYE SPEAK ABOUT HER husband and how important it was for Biff to cleanse his soul, Ariel goes to her home. With the bishop's conversation still running through her mind, she sits at the desk in her late husband's room and sips from her coffee cup. The soft, pale light of the full moon peeps inside her house through the bedroom window. As she glances up at the dark blue sky with twinkling stars scattered all across the expanse, she can't help but stare at the magnificence and perfection of the full moon. Then a thought enters her mind. She picks up her mobile phone and dials a number quickly, as if on some secret mission. After waiting for a couple of seconds, Ariel speaks, "Well, hello, my friend. How are you? Guess the kids are enjoying their spring break?"

"Yeah, I didn't expect to get a call from you. Are the kids all right? Is something wrong, Ariel?" asks Cassandra. "Oh no, I'm sure they are fine. You know no news is always good news. They only call us if there is something wrong," says Ariel. Then she continues, "Listen, Cassandra, I know we have never seen eye to eye on what it is you do, but I'd be willing to have my paper do a feature on your business if you come by my house tonight. I need a favor, please," requests Ariel with all her heart. After speaking over the phone for some 20 minutes, Ariel hangs up. She then walks into her living room and feels as if a huge burden has been lifted off her shoulders already.

Suddenly, the doorbell rings. Ariel greets Cassandra at the front door and thanks her for visiting on such short notice. Cassandra, donned in a purple and black dress, wearing black elbow-length silk gloves, rolls in a large suitcase. As she comes inside, Ariel notices that her glossy red lips become prominent against her pale skin.

Once they are both done exchanging their hellos, Cassandra says, "Let's go into your dining room, honey. I want you to bring every candle you own into the dining room. I have more in this second bag. Remember, we need to light 1,666 candles. You start on that and direct me to the last room your husband was in when he left home, like the bedroom, bathroom or if he left a coffee cup."

Like an obedient child, Ariel places and lights candles throughout the dining room, writing down on a notecard every candle she lights. Cassandra walks into the couple's bathroom looking for male items like deodorant, toothbrush, hairbrush, and other similar articles. She rambles through the dirty laundry, picking up and smelling soil men's, socks, and underwear, and places them in her black leather pouch. "Finding everything you need?" asks Ariel. Coughing from sniffing her husband's underwear, Cassandra replies, "Yes, sure, just keep lighting those candles, honey."

Cassandra walks into a room full of dancing candles moving back and forth. "Looks nice. Ah yes, the energy flow is good, Ariel," says Cassandra. As they sit at the dining room table, Cassandra pulls out her large iPad and mounts it on a stand. "I'm sorry, but what does this have to do with our call?" asks Ariel, bewildered. "Please, honey, sit down. We don't have a lot of time," says Cassandra. "Okay, but before we begin, let me just say this; I apologize for not respecting you as being a trained psychic medium. I have studied your work and know that you attended Arthur Findlay College in England, their school for psychics. I'm so sorry at the time I was too closed-minded to listen," says Ariel.

"Now, here we are, honey. You don't need to apologize. I'm here not just for you, but for us. As I said, sit down, please," says Cassandra with a comforting smile etched on her face. Turning on her iPad, the two observe a night video of the school. They see light flashes in the school windows, hear banging and loud screaming along with huge red blood splatters on windows. They also see a large ghostly figure walking between classroom school windows and are stunned by its energy and quick speed. Tears stream down Ariel's face as she continues to watch in shock. With her hand over her mouth, Ariel shakes her head, realizing it's none other than her own husband. At once, she starts reflecting on the words written in Biff's diary.

"After we spoke, I went to the school hoping I would get in, come back, pick you up, and we do our spirit ex-communication there, but the doors will not open," says Cassandra slowly. She continues, "A simple crowbar from my car will not work on the doors. I threw bricks at the window, but they flew back at me, knocking me to the ground. Trust me when I say this, Ariel—the screams are worst in person. This kid named Alex works there; my daughter Marie used to date him. She said they were going camping together…" stops Cassandra midway, as if immersed in some thought. "Let's just call the police. The sherriff is a good friend of mine. I'll text him now," says Ariel.

Cassandra spreads out Biff's personal items used the morning he left the house for work at Palmyra High. Two pair of black soil socks, his hair from his comb, one pair of dirty underwear, his toothbrush, and the last coffee cup that he drank from on his last breakfast, which had remained untouched on the table in his room.

"Before we get started, listen carefully. Your husband, Biff's spirit, is 95 per cent connected to Palmyra High School and 5 per cent here to this house. I know he has been here a couple of times, but his spirit is more comfortable living in the place where he accidentally passed away. His spirit is tied to the school. It sounds like he is becoming more psychotic, almost incapable of rational reasoning because some school high school students caused his heart attack," Cassandra breaks down the details. She talks about his soul and all that troubles him. She explains how he has not gone to heaven or hell, "Your husband is stuck on Earth. He hasn't crossed over to the afterlife like all spirits do, Ariel," says Cassandra. "Biff tries to come home because his memories are good and is where he prefers to have his spirit dwell until he crosses over. Now that he realizes he's dead, he's traumatized over his sudden death and is taking it out on people entering the school at night."

Cassandra further explains Ariel's husband sounds like he is turning more violent, going out of control quicker than she had anticipated. "Look, I just want to put his soul, his spirit to rest, and I'm sure you want that too," continues Cassandra.

"Yes, I do. I want Biff to stop killing innocent people. It's not fair. I've tried a seance, I've prayed with Bishop Faye, I wear these Rosary beads so that everything goes back to normal. Believe it or not, but I've even spoken with Biff. He's cried out to my family for help. I just need you to put him out of his misery, Cassandra," says Ariel, on the verge of tears.

"I have a plan, but understand your husband is becoming very powerful. He has the powers of electromagnetic interference, he disturbs electronics, and he's invisible. His telekinesis powers' ability enables him to move things with his mind. He now teleports with the blink of an eye, morph through walls to different locations, and that's how he came here." After a pause, Cassandra continues, "His strength is supreme, much stronger than humans, and now he has super speed because, after death, ghosts possess the ability to move at incredible speeds. Biff has Astro perception. The longer he lives, the more he will start manipulating the environment like the elements of fire, water, electricity, and even changing temperature."

"So, what happens if we can't get rid of his spirit?" asks Ariel.

"Your husband's spirit will live on and become a disciple, a recruiter of souls for the death reaper. This is why I've decided we need to get in my car and drive to a location I noticed near the school. We can proceed only if you agree," says Cassandra. When Ariel nods, they both leave the house and drive off in Cassandra's purple SUV into the early morning.

Winds begin blowing dust, and soon fog appears, hitting the SUV as Cassandra and Ariel drive on unpaved gravel roads into pitch-black darkness. "Cassandra, why the hell are we going on these back-farm roads? There's no light, and look at my phone, no signals either! This is stupid, Cassandra. Let's turn around. For some reason, I'm not comfortable with this anymore," says Ariel.

"Honey, don't wet your panties. I know what the hell I'm doing. These gravel roads are going to lead us to a four-way section, a crossroad for our crossroad demon. I know it is bumpy as shit, but just keep your Catholic faith, rub those beads because we're going to need all that girl," replies Cassandra confidently.

The road is bumpy, and the temperature outside goes from 60 to 30. Within moments, it starts snowing. All of a sudden, the women notice a pair of piercing red eyes in front of them. Before they could understand what was happening, the dark human-like ghost with red eyes appears to stand in front of their drive. Cassandra starts swerving side to side, and Ariel, unaware of this creature, continues complaining about the danger. In their course, when Ariel finally looks away from Cassandra and straight ahead, she sees the oncoming face of her husband Biff's half-human half-monster ghost,

"Aha, Aha, no, no!" screams Ariel continuously. Cassandra screams, too, but doesn't let go of the steering wheel. She swerves the SUV, turns sideways, rolling on two left wheels, flips, and then turns several times violently on the dusty gravel road. All the while they scream, Ariel holds on to her Rosary beads. Ultimately, the tumbling stops, and they find themselves upside down. Coughing and partially covered in bloody scratches, the women look around. They notice they are alive, but not without injury. Cassandra has a skinny piece of glass stuck in her ear. "Cassandra, oh my god. Your ear. Your ear!" screams Ariel. "Honey, will you calm down? You're the one with the beads still around your neck. Hold on to the beads, do your prayer thing, and quickly pull this piece of glass out now," shouts Cassandra, losing her patience.

"Okay, okay, on the count of three. One, two, three," says Ariel. Cassandra screams, trying her best not to create a scene. She unbuckles and then rolls out of the SUV. In an instant, she rips off her shirt and stops the bleeding. Then she wraps her head, puts on a jacket, and tells Ariel to grab the other bag in the back. "We must keep going. Let's start walking on foot. By using my powerful military-grade flashlight, I'm sure we'll be okay," guides Cassandra.

The ghost dressed as a grim reaper is seen riding black horses with red eyes. He is holding the horses' straps in one hand and the black reaper hatchet in the other hand above their heads, heading toward the women. But the two women, unaware of this sight, ride through them as Cassandra walks with a large gold cross in front of her face. She walks at a quick pace in front of Ariel, as if in a trance, speaking in tongues that seem to be giving her otherworldly power. Ariel sprinkles white salt rocks on the ground. They walk ten miles east into the early morning sunrise in eye view of Palmyra High School.

"Stop, Stop, honey. We're here," says Cassandra. "Why here? The school is just ahead. I'm tired, too, but we have to keep going," says Ariel, thinking that Cassandra wants to take a breather. "No, look. Remember the crossroads I told you about? Well, we're here. Look, four directions on a gravel road. We stop here and summon your husband's spirit by digging a hole in the middle of these four points," says Cassandra. Ariel understands what Cassandra means. They dig a six-foot hole, and Cassandra dumps items gathered from Biff's laundry along with his other remaining personal items inside.

They fill the hole with salt, placing the thick 12-inch gold cross in the middle. Cassandra places seven large sage reaped leaves around the hole. She lights them, and within seconds, smoke fills the air. She stretches her hands to her side, tilting her head back, and speaks in tongues again while the sun rises in front of them, shining on their faces.

Boom! The Palmyra High School rooftop blows into the skies, bursting into flames. The women drop on the ground from exhaustion, completely drained, and remain motionless.

CHAPTER 19

The Aftermath...

A HUMID BREEZE FLAPS MY DEN WINDOW CURTAINS, sending my Jamaican coffee aroma brew through the room. While channel surfing, I stop at the local news channel, "A massive explosion shook buildings throughout the town of Palmyra. Authorities say Palmyra High school exploded, scattering debris on homes, buildings, and cars," says the reporter. "I saw debris falling through the sky, and I was almost eight miles away from the school," says an eyewitness.

"As you can see from this cell phone video, flames shot some 60 feet into the sky. I'm told the school should have been empty because students are on spring break so far. The only visible sign of anything being in the area is this dog collar with the name Chester engraved on this gold plate," says the reporter.

"Good heavens! No, not my Chester!" Tears begin streaming down my cheeks. Without thinking much, I hop into my car and drive to the dusty explosion scene frantically. There's a hot haze and smell of gas in the air. Firefighters are seen breathing with the assistance of oxygen tanks strapped on their backs. I find the reporter and blabber, "Oh my God, my dog, my dog! You had his collar on TV. Have you seen him? Have you seen my Chester?" The reporter turns around. There are tears all over my face, snot coming out my nose, my eyes are bloodshot from crying and the debris dust. "Sir, I gave it to the officer over there, but there was no sign of your dog. I'm sorry," says the reporter politely.

Car alarms and ringing ambulances can be heard in the background. The fire trucks speeding up and down various streets seem to be in a rush. Many homes collapsed from the school's exploding. Entire families were seen holding one another throughout a three-mile radius of the school. I can taste the scent of gas and dust floating. My eyes begin watering as I walk toward a neighborhood command center. I'm a mess crying, coughing, sneezing, but I'm not even ashamed. And why should I? It's Chester we are talking about here. The dog I've treated as my own child. The animal who has always been by my side, like a loyal partner. I keep praying that Chester, my red Doberman, is still alive. God forbid if something were to happen to him, how would I be able to go on? He is my only family, and even the thought of him not being close by made my heart ache.

"Officer," I clear my throat, blow my nose, and continue, "This collar belongs to my Doberman named Chester. Any sign of him near here?" No response. I'm pushed aside, told to clear the area, and make way for cadaver dogs. They believe more dead bodies can be found.

I'm pacing back and forth with sweaty palms and a dry mouth, trying to keep my emotions intact and attempting to think positive thoughts. I pull out a cigarette to calm my nerves, but before I know it, this pale hand takes it out of my mouth. It's the chief of police. "What the fuck is wrong with you, professor? They stopped the gas leak, but there are still lots of fumes in the air," says the Chief.

"There is no crime in being anxious," I tell the chief.

"Anxious? Do you know something about this explosion that we don't?" Then after a brief pause, he continues, "I'm cuffing you, taking you to the police station for questioning."

"No, sir, see my dog's collar was found near the explosion,"

"What's he doing all the way over here? I should write you a citation for not having him on a leash, endangering my citizens. Serves him right," says the chief.

He walks off while talking on his police radio. Soon, loud barking echoes throughout the explosion area. The cadaver dogs appear to have located either body parts, tissue, blood, or bone from something. Unleashed German Shepards send police officers running behind them in almost six inches of debris. Apparently, they picked up a strong scent. They ignore dust haze honing on something.

Even firefighters refocus their attention on the dogs' frantic pursuit. The debris causes some officers to fall; it's so thick the dogs hurl themselves to one point near the school. They stop and start barking uncontrollably. Officers grab their mouths as some become nauseous. They all draw their guns suddenly as two unusually large white bats emerge from the thick white ash and school brick and glass explosion rubble. Gunshots ring in the air, and the mysterious white bats explode in the air in a cloud of smoke. Dogs that were barking till now suddenly stop. "Good boys, good job," says one of the police officers.

The coroner drives up and wheels out two black bags. By this time, everyone has on hazmat suits, which I found quite odd. As they load the bags and wheel them past me, I question, "Hey, what was identified over there?" Frustrated, I literally grab the arm of the coroner. He replies, "Listen, guy, skeletal remains of a large dog, guts, and human flesh, you happy now? Let go of my arm before I have you arrested, sir."

I stand there numb, weeping, walking toward my car in total disbelieve. My Chester of 12 years is gone. Disheartened, I try unlocking the door of my car with my remote door opener, but nothing happens. I try my key, but it won't budge. Then weirdly, the windows turn black, right in front of my eyes. In a panic, I step back and trip over the edge of the sidewalk, dropping my keys but never taking my eyes off the car. Looking around to see if anyone is noticing what I'm seeing, I get off the ground, and now, my windows are normal. My heart is thumping rapidly in my chest. Once again, I put the key in and open the door. This time, it opens. But before getting in, I bend, overlooking inside and make sure everything is all right. "Phew, all is clear," I say. After getting inside, I close the car door, snap my seat belt, and start the car. While blowing my nose, I put my foot on the gas. Pulling out on the street, I immediately slam on the brakes. The gas paddle felt extremely over-sided. It was because the janitor's composition book was neatly positioned over the gas paddle. As I picked it up, I notice there is explosion debris and blood on the book. Knowing this guy, the ghost of Biff the janitor who always wrote his last gruesome acts, I threw the book on the passenger side and pulled off towards home. Despite my car's windows rolled up, the pages begin flipping front to back nonstop, but since I do not want to stop, I pick up my speed. Distracted by the whole event, I end up running a speed light. Blue lights reflect in my rearview mirror, and I pull over. An officer walks up, and guess what, it's the same freaking chief. I look over the book and notice it is all calm, not moving at all.

"Professor, you sure have a nose for getting yourself in a pickle. Don't you? Or do you just have a jail fetish?" asks the chief.

"No excuses, no complaints, officer. I'll take the ticket. I am still upset over losing my Chester and could not focus on the light."

"Aw, lost bow-wow, didn't you? Here, take this ticket. It's $50. Make sure you pay it. I don't want to have to put you back in jail for not paying a moving violation. You have a good day you here," says the police chief.

Trying my best to stay composed, I pull back on the road, and as soon as I do that, the pages start moving from front to rear of the book. They continue to flip the entire time I drive, which was at least five miles. As I pull into the garage, this godawful odor and a gray-ish-colored liquid seep out from the book's spine. I get my garden work gloves and a garden hoe. I open the passenger door, use the hoe, and pulling the composition book on the floor; I scoop it up with my shovel. I pick up the book, sit it on my workbench, and read and read and read. *Oh my God! No!*

* * *

From a distance, a group of high school students can be seen preparing to dock their boat at a campground filled with cabins.

Honking sounds come from a black SUV Tahoe. Loud ear-deafening rock music seems to be shaking the entire vehicle. Everyone inside is screaming, yelling, and waving arms out the window. Pulling up near the boat dock is Alex, Amelio, D'Angelo, and Marie, who meet up with a few more friends at the camping grounds.

"What the hell took you guys so long to get here? Spring break is almost over!" says Sharron, one of the girls with group one.

"Well, yeah, long story. Believe me, you don't want to know. But hey, we're here now. Let's dock out boats and catch some fish before sundown," says Alex.

"We got beer, weed, and tequila," chimed in Bruce, the party starter of all the friends.

"Damn yawl. Sounds like more than spring break. Sounds like a celebration!" says D'Angelo, trying his best to get into the party spirit.

"Yeah, I guess you can call it that after what it took to finally get here," says Alex, looking at D'Angelo and then Marie and Amelio. The first crew works to ease the first boat into the lake. Sharron hops on to take control of the boat. It slides off the rack, but tilts into the water, sucking in the engine. "Hey, get Sharron out. The boat is sinking," shouts Bruce. Sharron dives in the water, the boat floats back up but is now unusable. They pull it in and leave it the way it is. Everyone gets in Alex's boat, determined to finish their spring break and have fun together. Drinking, smoking, laughing, water skiing, they end the day catching several fish.

On the way back in, Ted, a school classmate from the original boat, wants to know what took them four days to get to the campsite. The horizon is orange as the sun sets, casting an orange glow on the lake water. They look above and see two bats flying that swoop very close to their heads.

"Shit, dude, crank up that motor, so we don't get bit by them bats," says Ted. Alex turns the key, tries cranking the boat but realizes it's going nowhere. "Shit, man, it's going to be sunset soon. We got to get out of here, so we don't get kicked out of the campgrounds," says Alex. The engine starts but only accelerates at half the speed. A bat flies low, hitting Sharron in the head, and gets tangled in her hair. Losing her balance, Sharron falls in the lake. Alex cuts the motor, and the group members throw a life raft out, but she can't reach it. Still tangled in the top of Sharron's hair, the bat squeals, flaps its wings, and finally rips from her hair but not without taking a chunk of her blond hair with it in his mouth, flying and squealing into the horizon. Ted jumps in to help Sharron. Now Ted and Sharron are being pulled into the water. They struggle popping up, screaming, "Help, help!"

Behind the boat is a short island 10 x 10 in size. Alex looks behind him and is shocked to see a tall man's ghostly image and a pointed-eared dog with no tail looking at him. Alex's eyes widen, seeing the dog has blond hair hanging out of his mouth. His heart beats wildly as the horrors of the Palmyra High School start dominating his mind.

Maybe the nightmare is still not over. Perhaps, it never will.

-THE END-

ACKNOWLEDGMENTS

Outside of witnessing my two sons' birth, this acknowledgment makes the lump in my throat swell. It brings tears to my eyes because the absolute best friend in my life, the one human being that gave me birth and took my deepest hopes, dreams, and secrets to heaven, is the sole reason I am blessed to articulate today. Looking back to age four, I recall my mom singing and reading books to me late at night, capped off with a warm glass of milk. One of the scariest moments in my life was when I lost my voice after having my tonsils removed at the age of seven. Unable to speak, I could only ring a bell, and that whole incident left me in tears. But my mom was there, reading my favorite *Hardy Boys* mysteries, finishing with giving me a popsicle before going to sleep.

As a child, I remember spending many late-night hours in the back of my mother's graduate school classrooms, reading mystery books. I often stretched out on plush leather sofas in the large glass study rooms overlooking Michigan Avenue at Roosevelt University in Chicago, Illinois, while enjoying reading fictional mystery books. My mother, June Rice Newby Bacon, is the reason I can express my inner creative thoughts and feelings as the author of this novel and the future novel I am writing. I continue to write and study groups as my mother encouraged my younger brother and me to understand the relevance of fear pertaining to the unknown, even with the cultural and social issues.

Mom was an avid reader, a researcher, and behaviorist who dedicated her life to the observation of behavior related to people as well as animals, which is why she allowed me to purchase with my newspaper route money a squirrel monkey from the Zare Department store in Chicago, Illinois, in the late 1960s. While most parents would freak out, mom's love of pets and the exploration of behavior saw this as a behavioral learning and teaching moment for me and a teaching opportunity for her. Mom loved the theory of behavioral psychology, understanding the development of learned behavior through interactions in a particular environment. She believed everyone is a product of their environment.

Mom's influence on communication and articulation was fueled by encouraging me to produce a local radio show called *Horizons* while a freshman in high school, which aired on a Huntsville, Alabama, radio station, WEUP. She pushed me to study journalism at Columbia College in Chicago, which led me to work as a television news journalist in three major broadcast news network affiliate television stations. Mom convinced me to raise the money to purchase the rights to a radio broadcasting construction permit for radiofrequency 730 AM in Madison, Alabama, which I named WDKT, currently WUPM.

Upon my mother's death, I dedicated my continued education to obtain a master's in behavioral psychology and use my creative knowledge and education skills to tell engaging, often controversial fictional stories that amuse people as much as they fascinate me. My mother is a product of the historically Black university, Alabama A&M University. Mom earned a degree in English, including a double master's degree in Psychology and Sociology. My mom is my hero next to God; she gets all the glory.

Special thanks to Rob Heiden for
his support of Ghost of Palmyra High